Brews
and
Stilettos

Robert Chudnow

DEDICATION

Thank you to my lovely wife Teri for her patience and support. Without her this book would still be floating around in my mind and not in the pages that follow.

CONTENTS

ACKNOWLEDGMENTS

Many thanks to all who have helped me with
research and advise in writing this book.
Special thanks to:
My dear friend Phil Mandel for his council.
Dr. Sudeep Chandra for his information on Mongolia.
My brother David for his vast knowledge of Belgian Beers
and for introducing me to Lucky Baldwin's in Pasadena.

1 THE EXCHANGE

Timothy stashed the bag with his monk's clothing behind the boisterous bar. He was amazed at how good it felt to be back wearing jeans, his Stanford sweatshirt, and Nikes after a month wearing a monk's garb and sandals. He had even tried to hide his innocent demeanor with a fake tattoo on his arm. Feeling nervous about his upcoming meeting in the bar, he reached into his pocket for what must have been the fiftieth time to shake the leather pouch containing the one hundred two-carat diamonds he had and felt their reassuring rattle. He had left his motorbike half a mile from the bar to avoid any unwanted attention because he wasn't sure who would be keeping an eye on the bar.

For all the on-again, off-again dealings he and his father had over the years, this was certainly the most bizarre. He planned to bribe an older monk into giving him some secret information for which his father was willing to spend five million dollars in jewels. He had posed as a potential novitiate in a monastery outside Brussels for the last month just to set up this meeting. He did not know the reason for all the secrecy, but knowing his father, he figured there would be something dangerous involved.

As he got to the door, music and patrons spilled out onto the street. Timothy still wasn't used to the typical Belgian bars, especially compared to the quiet of the monastery he had been immersed in for the last month. He ordered an Orval beer at the bar and surveyed his fellow customers. It wasn't hard to spot the older monk in the back of the bar, even though he too had shed his monk's robes. The monk wore a stocking cap to cover his shaved head.

Timothy paid for his beer and went to the back to meet Brother Adolphus.

"Pleased to meet you, Mr. Daniels. I am Samuel Cook from the US," Tim said as he had been told.

The old monk still had a keen look about him and gave Tim a cautionary glance, but kept his alert eyes toward a group of rough-looking patrons to their right. Tim noticed the language they spoke was not Flemish or French as one would expect in a bar outside Brussels.

"Nice to meet you, Mr. Cook," said the monk.

Tim could sense something was not quite right and decided their exchange wasn't going to happen as planned. Instead, he and the monk drank their beers and made small talk about Brussels and Belgian beers. Fortunately, Tim was well schooled in both. After what seemed an interminable amount of time, the monk got up.

"Well, Samuel, it has been nice talking with you, but I think it is time to go." The monk's eyes darted to a large man sitting on the corner barstool. "Can I walk you to your car?"

Tim took the lead. "Yes, I think that would be fine. Perhaps I can give you a ride."

The hedge was like a whole forest as I
squeezed through. Those damp branches felt
like bony fingers against my arms. Halfway
through, I made a mistake. I turned and
looked back. Now the burnt house looked
different. Awful. Like some terrible night-
mare come true.

Then the barking started.

I'm not afraid of dogs. Not of dogs I can
see. But I couldn't *see* anything and all I
could hear was this howling and howling

coming out of the dark shadows. Was it one dog or a whole pack of them?

The barking wouldn't stop.

"Shut up!" I screamed. "Shut up! Shut up!"

But the howling noise went on, getting louder until it seemed to be coming from all sides at once. Was the dog over there? Or over there? I couldn't tell.

"You shouldn't have done this," the mother-voice, sister-voice told me. "You were stupid to go downtown alone. And stupid to try to walk home."

As I stood there, shivering, something covered with white hair jumped out from behind a parked car. A barking dog. I knew that dog. It was Jamal—only Jamal, the Michaelsons' bull terrier. There was no need to be afraid of him. Especially now when it was too dark to see his little pink-looking eyes and droolly jaws. No need to be afraid . . . except . . . except . . . Jamal was *never* allowed outside

alone. "Why?" I wondered. "Why?"

"Stupid," said the mother-sister voice.

Besides Jamal, all I could see were shadows. Pulling at me, holding me, choking me. I was never going to make it. Never going to get home.

I started to cry.

Then I heard another voice. Talking out loud. It was me. "Run," said the voice. "Run, you dummy. You're almost there."

So I ran. Like some crazy windup toy. My

feet were pounding and my heart was beating in my ears. "Keep going," that Tad-voice said. "Don't stop now."

At last—there it was. My apartment. If I could just reach the light by the front door, I'd be safe. Two at a time, I leaped up the steps.

Then, pushing open the door, I stepped in and slammed it behind me. I was at home. I'd made it.

Dad was in his chair reading and he looked up. "So where were you?" he asked. That was all. I felt better already.

I took a deep breath, but before I could answer Dad, my sisters came running in.

"Where did you go?"

"What happened? Are you all right?"

"Why didn't you tell us where you were?"

"It's after seven-thirty. Don't you know you're too young to be out after dark?"

When they were all finished asking their

questions, I answered. "Boys *are* allowed," I said.

"What?" they asked. "What's that supposed to mean?"

But I didn't say any more. I just went to find Ma. She was in the kitchen holding the telephone tight against her ear.

The minute she saw me, she started yelling things into the phone. "He's back! Tad's back! He's home!" Then she hung up and tried to hug me.

"Here," I said, wiggling out of her arms. "Happy birthday, Ma. I used all my money and I had to walk home from downtown."

"You walked home?" my sisters said. "From downtown?"

I looked up and saw Dad standing in the doorway of the kitchen. He winked at me. "Your mother and sisters are such worriers," he said. "I told them you were all right."

Ma opened the bag and pulled out the glass flower holder. She looked happy when she saw the way it shone in the kitchen light. It didn't have any card saying, "From T. C. Sharp IV," but she didn't seem to care.

"It's beautiful, Tad," she said. "Just look how beautiful. We shouldn't have been worried but we were. Are you all right?"

I heard what she was saying, but I didn't pay too much attention. I was home. I was safe.

Ma leaned over toward me. "Did anything happen, Tad? Is there anything you want to tell us?"

I looked up. Maybe I wanted to tell them how it was walking home. My stomach still felt funny when I thought of that walking and the dark world outside. But I wasn't going to do it. I wouldn't tell. Not one word.

So I just said, "No, nothing happened. Nothing at all."

Then I asked for a peanut-butter sandwich.

SUSAN TERRIS received her B.A. at Wellesley College and her M.A. in English Literature at San Francisco State College. She has written many books for children, including *The Drowning Boy; On Fire; The Upstairs Witch and the Downstairs Witch; Amanda, the Panda, and the Redhead; The Backwards Boots; Plague of Frogs;* and, most recently, *Whirling Rainbows.* Mrs. Terris and her husband, David, a stockbroker, live in San Francisco with their three children, Danny, Michael, and Amy.

RICHARD CUFFARI'S main interest in life is "making pictures." Since his graduation from Pratt Institute in Brooklyn, he has illustrated over eighty books, garnering along the way accolades from the Society of Illustrators, the American Institute of Graphic Arts, the Children's Book Council Showcase Exhibit, the Christopher Award, and several others. Born in Brooklyn, New York, Mr. Cuffari still makes his home there.

Inscribed especially
for my friend

Gene Tonekay

Best personal Wishes

H.H. Thomas

7 - 3 - 93

The Story of Allen and Wheelock Firearms

ALLEN'S IMPROVED ARMY PISTOL.

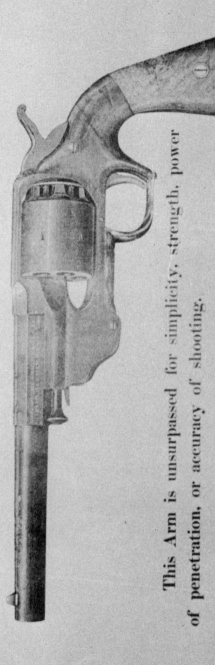

This Arm is unsurpassed for simplicity, strength, power of penetration, or accuracy of shooting.

Barrel, 7½ inches long; 44/100 Bore; 28 long, or 48 round Balls to the pound.

For loading, set the lock at half cock. The guard is used for a lever to drive the ball. To carry it safely when loaded, let the hammer rest between the nipples, or at half cock. To insure accurate shooting, and prevent leading the barrel the balls should be well greased and the Pistol kept clean. Use good SPERM OIL and SOFT LEAD.

ALLEN & WHEELOCK.
Worcester, Mass.

THE STORY

of

ALLEN AND WHEELOCK

FIREARMS

By

H. H. Thomas

Gun Collector, Lexington, Ky.

Preface by

Harold L. Peterson

Printed in the United States of America

by

THE C. J. KREHBIEL COMPANY
Cincinnati, Ohio

1965

This Work is Dedicated
To My Wife
Carolyn Who
Has No Love for Firearms
But Who Has Tolerated
My Interest In Them And
Has Traveled Many Miles
With Me In Pursuit Of
These Weapons

Collection of Kenneth Wyatt

Civil War Soldier Armed with
Allen & Wheelock Revolver,
Bowie Knife, Sharps Carbine,
Cavalry Saber

Preface

Every student of firearms has heard of Ethan Allen. Most are generally acquainted with his famous pepperbox pistols. Few, however, are aware of the tremendous range of guns which he made during the various partnerships he formed with one or another of his relatives. Fewer still have ever had the opportunity of seeing a comprehensive collection of the wide variety of models produced by Allen. Thus H. H. Thomas has performed a major service to all collectors and students by his compilation of this series of firearms made by Allen and Wheelock. As a result of his years of diligent search and study the rest of us may now look through this volume and learn quickly of the scope of Ethan Allen's work during this one partnership. It is an educational experience gained easily because of his efforts, and I, for one, am grateful for it.

Harold L. Peterson

Foreword

Having long been interested in the many variations of the Allen & Wheelock line of guns, I have searched diligently through stacks of old gun catalogues at numerous collectors' meetings and antique shops trying to find some listing of these guns. I have yet to find any reference to them except in current antique dealers catalogues. It's very hard to understand why there is next to nothing in print on these guns.

The intention of this book is to make the way a little easier for the new collector who may become interested in this fascinating line of firearms. I believe by picturing my collection, some friends collections and single pieces, that this book will cover all models and variations of this rare group of guns produced a hundred years ago at Worcester, Massachusetts.

From my belief that the specialist can build the most diversified collection under one brand name, comes this book.

These guns were produced prior to and during the Civil War; actually Ethan Allen and Thomas P. Wheelock manufactured firearms from 1856 through 1865. A period of 9 years through which these brothers-in-law produced the largest number of variations of firearms manufactured in the same period of time. Their plant was located at Worcester, Massachusetts.

These guns were manufactured in percussion, lip fire and rim fire, center hammer, side hammer and bar hammer with some of the most unique ejection and tamping systems known to man, also in all practical calibers of that period.

Having been collecting the variations of these Allen & Wheelocks for several years, my interest has been sparked by the relatively low serial numbers on all models. All the pistols in the author's collection have serial numbers of three digits or less. I know that any reader of this book will have enough interest in firearms to know how scarce the "Colt Walker" is, records indicate there were approximately 1000 produced; less than one hundred are accounted for today. Now in the light of this scarcity, consider the Allen & Wheelock where each model was evidently produced in quantities under 1000 each.

Having visited approximately thirty gun shows per year for the last decade, I have seen less than one-half dozen of several models of the Allen & Wheelock pistols. To name a few, the 8″ bbl. percussion side hammer navy model, the brass frame spur trigger rimfire revolver, the double barrel percussion pistol with single trigger, the double barrel shotgun of which I have seen only one, and the lipfire revolving rifle.

All revolvers of this manufacture are single action except the bar hammer type which are double action, including the single shot pistols.

Cased Allen & Wheelock's are a real rarity, the double cased pair, shown in this volume, was purchased by the author at the late George Walton's sale in Roanoke, Virginia. This is the only double casing I have observed. The label in the lid reads "Onion & Wheelock, Manufacturers and Importers of Guns, Pistols, Gun Material, Sporting Apparatus, No. 99 Maiden Lane, New York." As of this date, I have no information of the Onion associated with this name. These pistols are No. 197 & 203, the ivory grips are monogramed both sides of each grip, they are .22 cal. seven shot with 3″ barrels, marked "Allen & Wheelock, Worcester, Mass. U.S. Allens Patent Sept. 7, Nov. 9, 1858."

Realizing there are many pistols bearing the Allen name with other combinations of names this text will deal only with those marked Allen & Wheelock. There are pistols which show up at different collectors' meetings that closely resemble the Allen & Wheelock manufacture, although they bear no marking at all. I will leave these for speculation to others.

If there is anyone who would like to specialize in a challenging field of gun collecting, I am sure he would not be dis appointed if he chose to collect all of the models and variations marked Allen & Wheelock. I have been at it ten years and do not have them all yet. Some I have located but cannot buy, I can assure you that except for a few models of the desirable Colt, you will find hundreds of each variation and model to every one you will find by these two famous inventors.

H. H. Thomas

Acknowledgements

In the laborious task of locating and collecting materials on gunsmiths Allen and Wheelock and their associates, it has been my good fortune to have the constant and capable co-operation of various gun collectors and individual friends, as well as the help of several public institutions. Among the former, I must thank Jack Wilson, Marietta, Georgia; H. R. Mouillesseaux, Franklin Lakes, New Jersey; W. B. Sisler, Portland, Oregon; Charles Fritz and William Locke, Cincinnati, Ohio; Charles Worman, Dayton, Ohio; James F. Moser, Jr., Orange, Virginia; Dr. H. A. Brocksmith, Tulsa, Oklahoma; James F. Howard, Jacksonville, Florida; C. Meade Patterson, Hyattsville, Maryland; John Miller, Palm Springs, California; Clarence A. Collette, La Crescenta, California; John N. Peekering, Norfork, Virginia, and Walter D. Woodford, Cleveland, Ohio.

To those who aided me with historical and technical data on guns and gunmaking my warmest thanks and appreciation are due J. A. Visbeck, City Museum, Worcester, Massachusetts; Marcus A. McCorison, Librarian, American Antiquarian Society, . Worcester, Massachusetts; T. E. Hall, Winchester Gun Museum, New Haven, Massachusetts; John F. Beckness, Grafton, Massachusetts and Ivan Sandrof, Worcester, Massachusetts.

My particular thanks are extended to J. Winston Coleman, Jr., for reading and checking the manuscript; to Ted G. Osborne for photographic work, and to Mrs. Margaret Stone for preparing the manuscript for publication.

It is my hope that the reader may find something within these pages to bring back the life and deeds of Allen and Wheelock, two relatively obscure and fine gun makers who operated in Massachusetts during the middle years of the last century.

April 15, 1965
Paris Pike, R.R. 3   H. H. Thomas
Lexington, Kentucky

Contents

ETHAN ALLEN.

The Inventors Allen & Wheelock

In the past parade, for no known reason, certain men a long time dead, seem to emerge now and then as if summoned by Gabriel's trumpet. Such a man is Ethan Allen, a Worcester, Massachusetts inventor and firearms manufacturer, who died quietly at his home, 16 Murray Ave., on January 7, 1871, at the age of sixth-four.

He wore a thick brush of beard as was the fashion then. His eyes were keen and full of concentration. And even though he was no relation to the historical Ethan Allen of Green Mountain fame, his name was known throughout much of the world.

He is forgotten now. But gun collectors, a loyal and devoted breed of men who may not be able to hit the side of a barn door, but love the look and feel of a polished old weapon, know and revere Allen's name and accomplishments. Between 1845 and 1862 alone, he filed nine important patents, all of them dealing with firearms.

The most colorful chapter of Allen's life revolved about the Allen pepperbox, a fiery little weapon with a lot of "spice."

It became so famous that it made its mark in our literature. Sailing vessels carried it around the Horn and hearty prospectors crossed the isthmus of Panama armed with the pepperbox. Forty-Niners refused to go to the ore diggings without it. Emigrants liked its cold reassurance. Mississippi steamboat gamblers with a free-drawing "se-gar" in their mouths, stuck the sturdy little firearm in the waist sashes.

Writer Alfred T. Jackson, in a book published in 1920 called *Diary of a Forty-Niner*, wrote that: "Donovan . . . . jumped a claim, and when the rightful owner warned him off, he drew an Allen pepperbox."

Mark Twain did even better. In his book, *Roughing It*, he described in his humorous manner how one of the characters shot a tree-climbing buffalo with an Allen pepperbox   In telling of his anger when the story was questioned, the man said, "I would have shot that long gangly lubber they called Hank if I could have done it without crippling six or seven people, but of corse, I couldn't, the old Allen's so confoundly comprehensive."

Another amusing description of his experience with this self-cocking revolver, and the degree of skill in marksmanship which he had acquired by constant practice. "There was," he says, "no safe place in all the region round about." On one occasion, he brought down a cow fifty yards to the left of the target, and an interested spectator persuaded him to purchase the carcass.

Allen invented his pepperbox in 1834. He made it so it could fire four, five or six shots as rapidly as the trigger could be pulled. Previous to this weapon, most hand guns could fire only one shot at a time without reloading.

This placed a lot of reliance upon accuracy. What was sorely needed, however, was a quick gun for emergency use at close quarters; one that could be plucked from under a pillow, or snatched from a suitcoat when peril threatened. There was plenty of peril, too, in the old days, and it was rare for any traveler to go unarmed.

The rapidity of fire from the pepperbox made it the the fastest shooting iron of its day. Accuracy didn't matter nearly as much as fire power.

A Captain Walker wrote to Colt (the famous gunmaker) in 1847 that, "nine men out of ten in this city do not know what a Colt pistol is and although I have explained the difference between yours and the six-barrel Pop Gun that is in such general use a thousand times, they are still ignorant on the subject . . ."

The pepperbox came in various sizes from .28 to .40 caliber. The largest guns with the biggest bore were popular with the hard-riding military; they were called "dragoons." They spat fire in the Seminole War, the War with Mexico, the Civil War and were in use as late as 1867, when the U.S. Cavalry fought to subdue the Cheyennes.

Ethan Allen was born in Bellingham, Mass., on Sept. 2, 1808. He worked in a factory as a boy. At 21 he went out on his own in Milford, making cutlery on a modest basis. When he was 24, in 1832, he moved to Grafton, and set up shop in what was then called New England Village, it is now North Grafton.

Here Allen began making knives and tools for cobblers. His first venture into the manufacture of guns may have been in the form of a cane gun. "This sort of thing," declared an early account, was "desirable for nature lovers, naturalists and poachers."

What seemed like a harmless cane dropped its hollow shell at the press of a button and the handle became a firearm.

The cane gun sold so well that Allen was encouraged to do more. Soon after he settled in Grafton he formed a partnership with his brother-in-law, Charles Thurber.

In 1837, a succession of help wanted ads for gunsmiths ran in the *Worcester Palladium*. Apparently it brought few results. Lack of skilled employees and poor transportation were handicapping growth. Allen moved to Norwich, Conn., lock, stock and barrel.

The great fire of June 14, 1834, turned this building into shambles. The property was rebuilt, but Allen & Thurber decided to have their own mill and put it up near South Worcester station, a section called the Junction.

He returned to Worcester in 1845, to find plenty of help and transportation. Expanded quarters were found in the W. T. Merrifield building of four stories, in the square between Union and Cypress streets and Exchange and North Foster streets.

Allen's business was always a family set-up. About this time he admitted another relative, T. P. Wheelock into the firm, which became Allen, Thurber & Co., until 1857 when Thurber retired.

The men behind the trigger now became Allen & Wheelock, until Mr. Wheelock died in 1864. Allen went on to form a partnership with his two sons-in-law, Sullivan Forehand and H. C. Wadsworth, under the firm name of Ethan Allen & Co.

When Allen died in 1871 the business was continued as Forehand & Wadsworth. Forehand continued as head man after 1883 and when he died the business was bought by the Hopkins and Allen Arms Co., of Norwich, Conn.

But in between all this biggelty-pigglety of firm names, there's a lot of story.

The nation was growing like a balloon blown up by the wind of a giant. When you study the picture coldly, it's amazing how dependent expansion was upon guns. The settlers creaking west in Conestoga wagons carried them, the gold hunters carried them and the varmints carried them. There were more varmints than the law. Emigrants needed them. There was the military, the sheriffs, the deputy sheriffs, the posses, the vigilantes — and you take it from there.

Gun-makers capable of large production were needed to supply the demand. Allen, Thurber, Wheelock, Forehand, Wadsworth and others boomed on the need and became tremendously successful.

They made several other weapons besides the famous pepperbox. There were breech-loading rifles, double-barrel shotguns, muzzle-loading cartridge revolvers, single cartridge pistols, fowling pieces and other items.

The one biggest and most important item was the metallic cartridge. Such cartridges could not be made anywhere up to that point except by tedious, slow and expensive hand operations.

Allen made and patented the first machine for doing this. It caused a tremendous explosion throughout the world. The patent robbers saw a good thing and went sniffing and tearing at it with an expensive corps of legal beagles. They were held off.

At the Centennial Exposition of 1876, one observer wrote, "nothing in the mechanical line attracted more attention than Allen's astounding invention."

The Worcester firearms pioneer had gone into high gear at a point when one of the most important changes in firearms took place — the change from muzzle-loading to breech-loading guns. Right behind it came the change from loose to fixed ammunition — the type that is used today.

In 1864, a history of American manufacturers reported that "The Revolver and Rifle Manufactory of Allen & Wheelock is quite extensive."

With the Civil War already flaring at the edges, the local company was asked to submit a revolver for official use to a board of Army officers. Allen & Wheelock came up with their Army "Last Model," a 6-shot percussion system revolver of .44 caliber, single action, center hammer with blued metal finish and polished hardwood handles.

The Government ordered 500 of these, would have bought more. But Lincoln's agents scouting Europe for weapons found quite a few similar revolvers had been sold abroad and bought all they could get for the Union Army Volunteer officers.

By 1870, competition being what it was, the gunmakers began competing for the customer's dollar with low-cost guns that sold for about $2. Allen now had the bristling competition of Iver Johnson and Harrington and Richardson, Inc.

Out came a rash of pocket pistols, single action, hand-cocked, some with cheap engraving, some with bone handles. They sported names like Defender, Terror, Dictator, Blue

Jacket, Red Jacket, Chichester, Great Western and Tramps' Terror.

After a while they won the unofficial name of "suicide specials" because so many were found beside the bodies of suicides.

Ethan Allen piled up a fortune from his business. He lived in an imposing mansion, designed by Elias Carter, which is still standing at 770 Main Street as one of the best existing local examples of the Classical Revival period of architecture.

He moved from here to another white mansion which he had built on Murray Avenue. It was of the same architectural period, with six huge Corinthian pillars facing the front. The mansion dominated the Main Street area in this section like a baronial estate set in a lush emerald lawn. A fishpond where carp capered attracted the small fry.

A classic story is told about Allen's encounter with a crook in his first house. Hearing noises at night, Allen crept downstairs to find a pilferer loading up the family jewels, or at least the silver. The yegg heard him and whirled about with one of Allen's own guns. This was base ingratitude of the first degree.

But Allen with a reputation as a cold nerve, leaped upon the crook, disarmed him and gave him a thorough caning. Then he locked him in a closet until morning and went back to bed.

But he was too excited   The longer he lay in bed the angrier he got. Finally he stamped downstairs again, unlocked the closet, dragged out the protesting burglar and beat him again.

Allen was married twice. There were no children by his first wife. The *Worcester National Aegis* of Jan. 6, 1841, carried this legal notice: "Ethan Allen finds his wife Mary Allen impossible to live with and will not be responsible for her debts in the future."

On Jan. 12, 1843, Allen was married to Mrs. Sarah E.

(Murray) Johnson in Norwich, Conn. There were several children, but the only son, William Ethan, died Nov. 7, 1893, at 36. Mrs. Allen died on March 5, 1896 at 79.

At the funeral of the successful inventor and gun manufacturer, in 1871, the Rev. H. L. Wayland, a Baptist pastor and friend of the family paid high tribute to Allen. "All of his creations," he said in part, "were characterized by the extreme simplicity that seems one of the higher marks of a truly great inventor."

Allen's name, apart from his pistols, is perpetuated in Worcester by the old Ethan Allen mansion and by Ethan Allen Street which connects Murray and Jacques Avenue. It was so named in 1927.

The manufacturing plant was swallowed up by Crompton & Knowles Loom Works and is still standing as building number six in the vicinity of Gardner Street and the Boston & Albany Railroad in South Worcester. The old timers refer to this building as "the old pistol shop."

And so it goes.

From *Worcester Gazette*, January 9, 1871:

"Obituary of the Late Ethan Allen — Mr. Ethan Allen, widely known as an inventor and manufacturer of fire-arms, died at his residence in this city last Saturday, at the age of sixty-four. For the last twenty five years he has resided here, and his enterprise and talent have in no inconsiderable degree influenced the development of Worcester as an industrial and mechanical center. He was born and reared in Bellingham and began his business career in 1832, in Grafton, as a manufacturer of pocket cutlery and shoe tools. Soon after, he began the manufacture of pistols, and removed to Norwich, Conn., in 1837, where, in partnership with Mr. Charles Thurber, a brother-in-law, he continued business until 1845, when the firm removed to Worcester.

"About the time of this removal, Mr. Allen invented his first revolver, and from this beginning, he continued to produce new and improved arms, and machinery for their manufacture, till his name as an inventor and manufacturer of revolvers, breech-loading rifles and shot-guns became known throughout this country and Europe. The works of Allen and Thurber, in Merrifield's buildings, were destroyed in the great fire of June 14, 1834, and subsequently the present establishment near the Junction was erected, and the late Mr. T. Prentice Wheelock was admitted to the firm, the name being Allen, Thurber & Co. In 1837 Mr. Thurber retired and Allen & Wheelock continued the business till 1864, when the firm was dissolved by the death of Mr. Wheelock. Messrs. Sullivan Forehand and H. C. Wadsworth, sons-in-law of Mr. Allen, were subsequently admitted to the firm of Ethan Allen & Co., and under this name it has since continued.

"Mr. Allen's residence here has covered the most important period of the history of Worcester. He has seen it develop from a small country town, to a great manufacturing center, and by his energy and faithful devotion to business, he has kept his own enterprises advancing with the general growth, till he acquired a comfortable fortune. He has always been held in high esteem by his friends and business acquaintances, as a man of probity and honor; his devotion to his business and mechanical studies has kept him from an active participation in public affairs, but his general information and good judgment have rendered him a sound counselor to many who have sought his advice. His funeral will take place at 11 o'clock Tuesday morning."

Taken from the *Worcester Spy*, May 23, 1864:

"In this city on Saturday last (May 21, 1864) died of apoplexy, Mr T. P. Wheelock, of the firm of Allen & Wheelock. He was stricken down in the midst of health and usefulness, in his fifty-first year. He was a high minded and honorable man, and better than all, a whole-hearted Christian.

"The funeral will take place from the Main Street Baptist Church, on Tuesday, the 24th, at two o'clock P.M."

THE ETHAN ALLEN HOMESTEAD.

Chapter 1

Pepperboxes

These multishot firearms produced by Allen & Wheelock come in four, five and six shot, with barrel lengths from 2.5 to 6 inches long. In calibers: .28, .31, .34, and .36.

These are all double action and have bar hammers, usually with engraved frames and engraved cap shields fitted around base of barrels over the percussion nipples. Its purpose was to prevent loose caps from being lost and to prevent multiple firing by chain explosions when only one shot was intended.

The pepperboxes shown on the following plates bear the name Allen & Wheelock. However, it is evident from the patent dates that this line was patented long before Ethan Allen formed a partnership with his brother-in-law, Thomas P. Wheelock. It can be reasonably established, however, that they were discontinued at the end of the Allen & Wheelock partnership.

Ethan Allen obtained the first American patent for the double action pepperbox. This action involves pulling the trigger which revolves the barrel one position and raising the hammer simultaneously as the trigger is pulled fully back, releasing the hammer, and thus firing the gun.

There were enough barrels on the "ole" pepperbox that one was to be feared, even in the hands of an amateur. It was doubtless that, if he kept pulling the trigger, he would eventually hit the target.

The pepperbox won immediate acceptance by home owners and shop keepers because they did not have to depend on the first shot. The forty-niners used them to protect their claim and to ward off gold thieves. Dance-hall girls found them easy to conceal and a boost to their confidence. They were reportedly used by the United States Army in their fight with the Cheyennes in 1867.

Allen's array of kinfolk-partnerships include his brother-in-law, Thomas Prentice Wheelock, produced more pepper-boxes than most of his competitors combined. The Allens outsold Colt for nearly a decade. This firm was the first to use the double action system. Until this time, the hammer had to be cocked manually before the trigger could be pulled.

A humorous incident recounted by Mark Twain on his journey westward was the inaccuracy of the old pepperbox. He told of a stagecoach passenger who was shooting out of the stagecoach window. "He aimed at a duce of spades nailed to an oak tree, but felled the nearby mule, and although he had no desire to own the carcass, he was persuaded to purchase it."

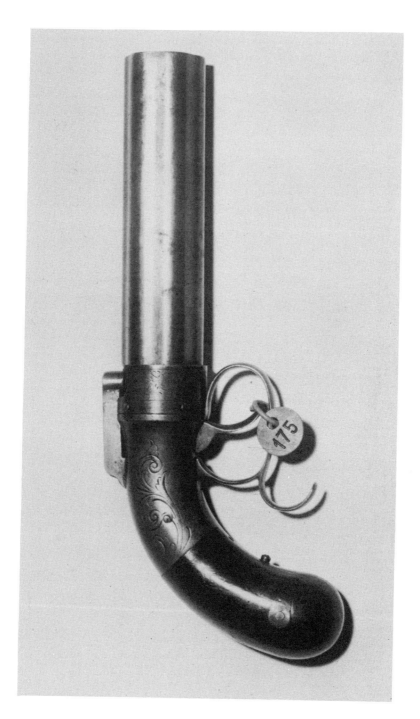

12

PLATE II

ALLEN & WHEELOCK PERCUSSION PEPPERBOX (dragoon)

Markings:
In barrel flute: ALLEN & WHEELOCK
Left side of bar hammer: PATENTED APRIL 16, 1845
Engraved, frame and cap shield

Caliber: .36
Barrel: 6" fluted
Number of shots: 6
Grips: Walnut varnished
Serial number: Unknown
Finish: Blued

13

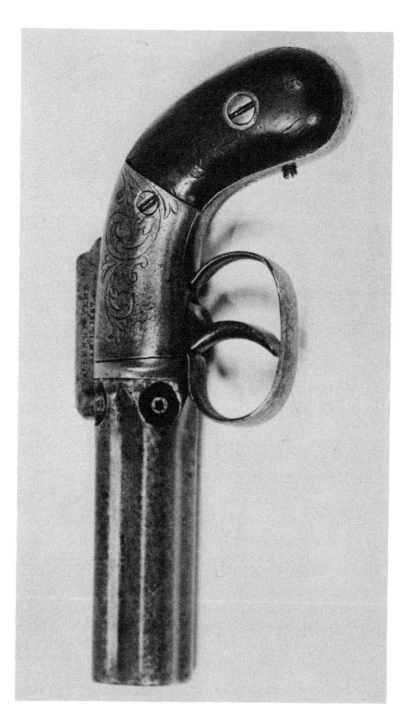

From Jack Wilson's collection

14

PLATE III

PERCUSSION PEPPERBOX

Markings:
In barrel flute: ALLEN & WHEELOCK
On side of hammer: Allen's patent Jan. 18, 1857
Engraved frame

Caliber: .31
Barrel: 2⅞″ fluted
Number of shots: 4
Grips: Walnut varnished
Serial number: 528 on major parts
Finish: Blued

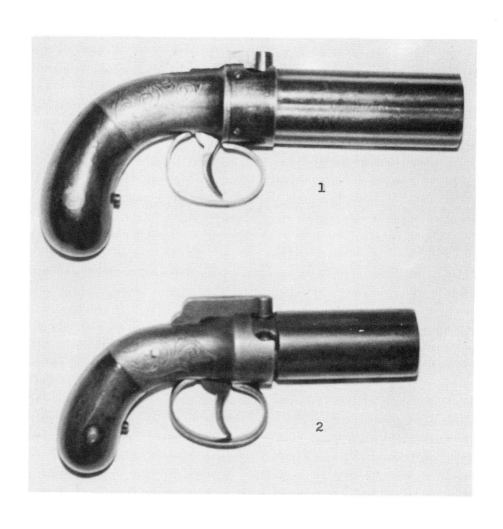

From the author's collection

PLATE IV

Fig. 1
PERCUSSION PEPPERBOX

Caliber: .31
Barrel: 2.5″ fluted
Number of shots: 5
Grips: Walnut, varnished
Serial Number: 4 on major parts
Finish: Blued

Markings:
In barrel flutes: Worcester Patented Apr. 16 ALLEN & WHEELOCK
On side of Hammer: Allen's Patent 1845
Distinctive feature: Frame and cap shield made in one part
Frame & side plate only: Engraved

Fig. 2
PERCUSSION PEPPERBOX

Caliber: .31
Barrel: 3.25″ fluted
Number of shots: 6
Grips: Walnut, varnished
Serial Number: 85 on major parts
Finish: Blued

Markings:
In barrel flutes: Worcester Patented Apr. 16 ALLEN & WHEELOCK
On side of hammer: Allen's Patent 1845
Engraved frame and cap shield

17

Chapter 2

Allen & Wheelock Pocket Model
Double Action Percussion Revolver

In the following plates you will see pictured six of the rare little gems. The bag type grips, hammer, frame and trigger guard all closely resemble that of the pepperbox. These are all equipped with octagon barrels, and in the characteristic low serial range. They all possess deep cut cylinder engraving showing a forest scene with wild animals, dogs and fowls.

All of this model observed by the author have the calibers .28, .31 and .34 with barrel lengths from $2^2/_8''$ to $3^7/_8''$.

Of these pictured the cylinder scene on the small caliber show ducks or geese, where the larger calibers show only animals — deer, dogs and so forth.

·Another variation of this model is the barrel marking, only serial 376 and 11 has the Allen & Wheelock on the top of the frame instead of the usual markings on the left side of barrel.

Still another variation is the means to remove cylinder pin serial numbers 376 and 11 (cased) the cylinder pin has a slot to receive screw driver where it projects through front of frame under the barrel. Removal of this pin releases the cylinder. The other four (pictured) have a screw in bottom of frame under barrel. By removing this screw the cylinder pin slides forward releasing cylinder. Also a groove on under side of barrel for top curve of cylinder pin to slide in.

18

It was surely the inventors' intention that this model was for close range as there is no provision for sights, either front or rear.

These were carried by many outlaws, who are often more interesting than in-laws, whose guns were not mere weapons, but true friends and won their greatest fame when "revolvers were revolving."

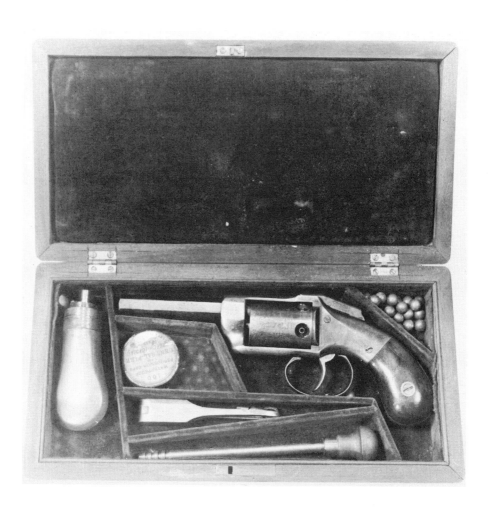

From Jack Wilson's collection

PLATE V

DOUBLE ACTION BAR HAMMER PERCUSSION POCKET MODEL

Caliber: .28
Barrel: 3½″
Number of shots: 5
Grips: Walnut
Serial number: 11 on major parts
Finish: Blued

Markings:
Top of frame: ALLEN & WHEE-LOCK
On left side of hammer: Patented April 16, 1845
Deep cut cylinder engraving of forest scene and animals

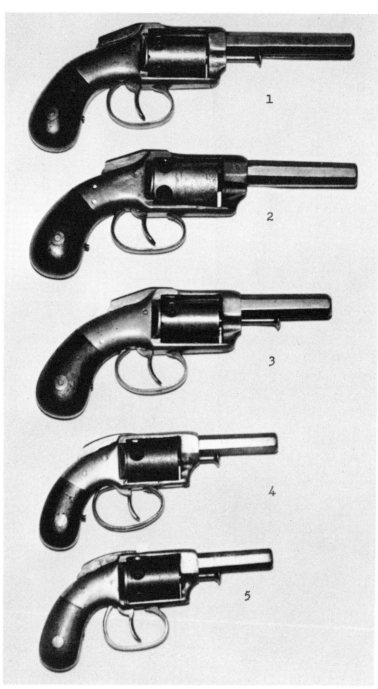

From the author's collection

PLATE VI

Fig. 1

DOUBLE ACTION, BAR HAMMER, PERCUSSION POCKET MODELS

Caliber: .34
Barrel: 3⅛"
Number of shots: 5
Grips: Walnut
Finish: Blued
Distinctive feature: Has ¼" recess between nipples for hammer rest

Markings:
On left side of barrel: ALLEN & WHEELOCK WORCESTER, MASS U.S.
Allen's patent April 16, 1845
On left side of hammer: Patented April 16, 1845
Deep cut cylinder engraving with forest scene and animals

Fig. 2

Caliber: .34
Barrel: 3⅝"
Number of shots: 5
Grips: Walnut, varnished
Serial number: 376 on major parts
Finish: Blued

Markings:
On top of frame: ALLEN & WHEELOCK
On left side of hammer: Patented April 16, 1845
Deep cut cylinder engraving with forest scene and animals

Fig. 3

Caliber: .34
Barrel: 2⅞"
Number of shots: 5
Grips: Walnut, varnished
Serial number: 659 on major parts
Finish: Blued

Markings:
On left side of barrel: ALLEN & WHEELOCK WORCESTER, MASS.
Allen's Patent April 16, 1845
On left side of hammer: Patented April 16, 1845
Deep cylinder engraving with forest scene and animals

Fig. 4

Caliber: .31
Barrel: 2½"
Number of shots: 5
Grips: Walnut, varnished
Serial number: 271 on major parts
Finish: Blued

Markings:
On left side of barrel: ALLEN & WHEELOCK WORCESTER, MASS.
Allen's Patent April 16, 1845
Distinctive features: no markings on hammer
Deep cylinder engraving with forest scene, two deer — buck and doe, ducks, cabin & lake

Fig. 5

Caliber: .31
Barrel: 2⅜"
Number of shots: 5
Grips: Walnut, varnished
Serial number: 387
Finish: Blued

Markings:
On left side of barrel: ALLEN & WHEELOCK WORCESTER, MASS.
Allen's Patent April 16, 1845
Distinctive features: no markings on hammer
Deep cylinder engraving with forest scene, two deer — buck and doe, ducks, cabin & lake

Chapter 3

Allen & Wheelock Bar Hammer, Single Shot Percussion Pistol

These pistols are also double action, part octagon to round barrels, some have engraved frames, some do not.

The single shot percussion pistols were probably made for the trade that could not afford the more elaborate revolving pistols.

We could surely assume that they were also popular with the Forty-Niners and were carried across the country to California during the gold rush days and were carried around the Horn on sailing ships. Some saw service in the Seminole War in Florida and the Mexican War and surely were a welcome companion to many a Civil War soldier.

Those examined by the author had barrel lengths from $2^5/_8''$ to $10''$ and calibers .31 and .36, made with screw-off barrel.

These weapons enjoyed their popularity during the un-hurried days of yesteryear when men's lives were spent in an atmosphere of tranquility of mind and serenity of soul: long before haste, turmoil and greed became dominant in the activities of men.

On December 12th, 1862 a part of the western flotilla of the Union Navy entered the Yazoo River at Vicksburg, Mississippi. Its purpose was to knock out the Confederate batteries that had been harrassing the movement of troops and supplies for several months.

Among this flotilla was the Union gun-boat *Cario* under Lieutenant Commander, T. O. Selfridge. About twelve miles up the Yazoo the *Cario* was hit by two Confederate torpedoes, one exploding under her bow the other under her quarter and the iron-clad sank in twelve minutes, disappearing completely, save the top of her smoke-stacks. The discipline of the crew was perfect, the men remaining at quarters until they were ordered to abandon ship and no lives were lost.

The old gun-boat has recently been brought to the surface and in the officers quarters there was found an old Allen bar hammer single shot percussion pistol — Plate VII-B, which has survived the watery tomb for a hundred and two years, and is shown on the accompanying plate, courtesy of Vicksburg National Military Park, Vicksburg, Mississippi. Note the unusually good condition of the walnut grips.

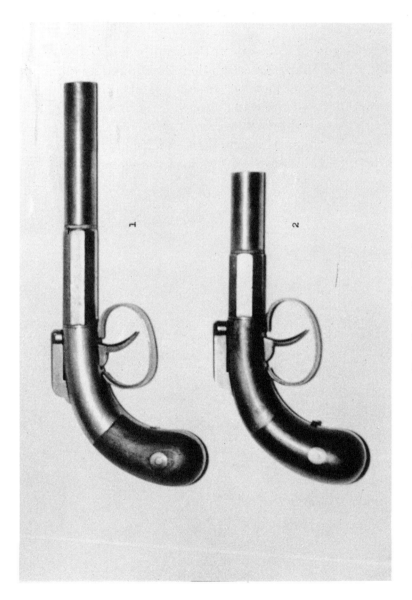

PLATE VII

ALLEN & WHEELOCK DOUBLE ACTION, BAR HAMMER, SINGLE SHOT, PERCUSSION PISTOL

Fig. 1

Caliber: .36
Barrel: 5"
Grips: Walnut, varnished
Serial number: 199 under barrel on each grip and frame
Finish: Blued

Markings:
  Top of barrel: ALLEN & WHEELOCK
  On left side of hammer: Patented April 16, 1845

Fig. 2

Caliber: .36
Barrel: 3"
Grips: Walnut, varnished
Serial number: 295 under barrel on each grip and frame
Finish: Blued

Markings:
  Top of barrel: ALLEN & WHEELOCK
  Distinctive feature: No markings on hammer

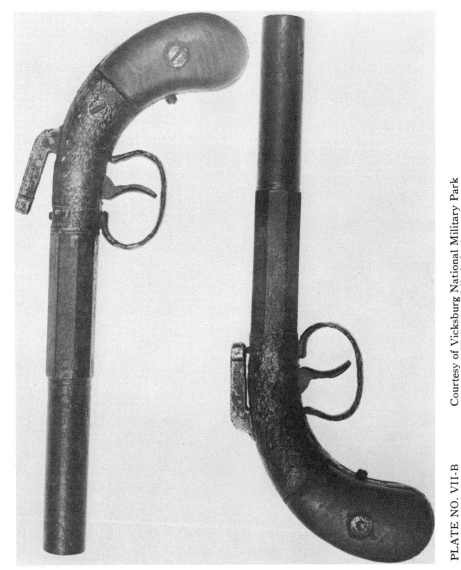

PLATE NO. VII-B   Courtesy of Vicksburg National Military Park
Vicksburg, Mississippi

Chapter 4

Allen & Wheelock Center Hammer, Straight Line Percussion Pistol

It is evident from this scarce model that the inventors were striving hard to stay in the market with the low priced competition. On this model they dropped the trigger guard, also produced a one piece frame without an inspection plate, squared up the grip butt, drilled straight through and inserted the percussion nipple directly behind and in straight line with barrel. Thus the name "Straight Line."

They were produced with the center hammer, spur trigger, single action. The barrel is octagonal except for a rounded section approximately one inch long on the rear bottom of barrel, which gradually offsets up about one sixteenth of an inch and becomes octagonal on to the muzzle.

The inventors did deem this one worthy of sights. The front one is German silver morticed into the barrel flat, the rear sight is a steel blade type grooved into octagonal section forming top of frame.

The serial numbers are located on the bottom of barrel, just forward of rounded section, also on the inside of each walnut grip and on the frame under the grip.

This speciman has been observed in barrel lengths from three inches to six inches.

During a recent conversation with a well known and reputable dealer he stated that he had only handled one of this model. The writer knows of no more than a half dozen.

The muzzle has the rounded beveled edge which is characteristic on many models bearing the Allen & Wheelock name.

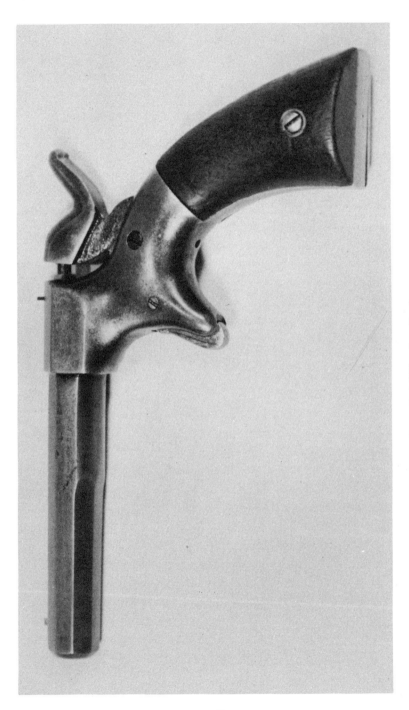

30

PLATE VIII

ALLEN & WHEELOCK CENTER HAMMER, STRAIGHT LINE, PERCUSSION, SINGLE SHOT PISTOL

Caliber: .31
Barrel: 3"
Grips: Walnut
Serial number: 132
Finish: Blued

Markings:
  ALLEN & WHEELOCK on left side of barrel
Distinctive feature: Percussion nipple forms straight line
  with screw barrel
Estimated number manufactured: Less than 500

Chapter 5

Allen & Wheelock Center Hammer, Percussion Pistols

The intention of the inventors must surely have been to extend their range when they introduced this model, because the barrel lengths were extended up to ten inches.

This model must have been well received as there seems to be rather good picking for the collector as compared to many of the other Allen & Wheelock models.

Have been unable to locate a patent date on this particular model, the serial number and the inventors' names being the only markings.

These pistols must have had a special appeal to the marksman of a century ago, also the pretentious bad man, for they could present a dreadful appearance with the long barrel and the larger caliber.

Although these are classified as the center hammer, the hammer is actually off center so as not to interfere with the aim. They are equipped with a brass bead front sight, and a raised V-slot located on top of frame at the rear end of barrel.

Of the six specimens pictured on the following plates, none are engraved, only a finely graduated section separating the octagon and round section of the barrel.

There is a small flash guard at the nipple which is an integral part of the frame.

The entire outward surface of this model exposes only two screw heads, one for the grips and one for the inspection plate on side of frame.

The walnut grips are neatly mortised to fit under frame and inspection plate.

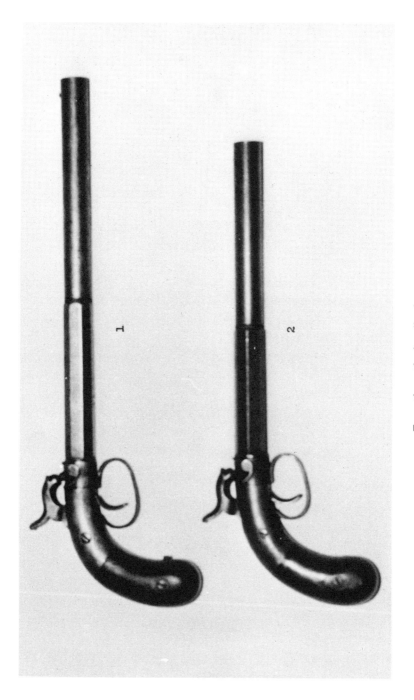

PLATE IX

CENTER HAMMER, SINGLE SHOT, PERCUSSION PISTOL

Fig. 1

Markings:
On top of octagon section of barrel: ALLEN & WHEE-
LOCK

Caliber: .36
Barrel: 10″
Grips: Walnut
Serial number: 524
Finish: Blued

Fig. 2

Markings:
On top of octagon section of barrel: ALLEN & WHEE-
LOCK

Caliber: .36
Barrel: 8″
Grips: Walnut
Serial number: 44
Finish: Blued

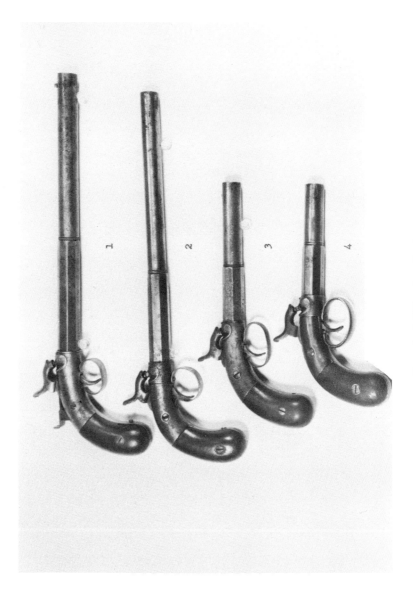

From Jack Wilson's collection

PLATE X

CENTER HAMMER SINGLE SHOT PERCUSSION PISTOLS

Fig. 1

Markings:
On top of octagon section of barrel:
ALLEN & WHEELOCK
Distinctive features: Back strap cut for shoulder stock and peep sight.

Caliber: .34
Barrel: 10"
Grips: Walnut
Serial number: 228
Finish: Blued

Fig. 2

Markings:
On top of octagon section of barrel:
ALLEN & WHEELOCK

Caliber: .36
Barrel: 9¾"
Grips: Walnut
Serial number: 322
Finish: Blued

Fig. 3

Markings:
On top of octagon section of barrel:
ALLEN & WHEELCOK

Caliber: .44
Barrel: 5"
Grips: Walnut
Serial number: 21
Finish: Blued

Fig. 4

Markings:
On top of octagon section of barrel:
ALLEN & WHEELOCK

Caliber: .36
Barrel: 4"
Grips: Walnut
Serial number: 175
Finish: Blued

37

Chapter 6

Allen & Wheelock Double Barrel, Single Trigger Pistols

Any gun collector can truthfully testify that this speciman will not be found in groups.

The two barrels are cast from one piece of steel with a flute both top and bottom between barrels. It has a German silver bead front sight with the space between the two hammers forming the rear sight.

The two exposed screws for the inspection plate and grips enter from the left side on this model. Due to the two hammers this model has an inspection plate each side.

The serial numbers are located in bottom flute of barrel, on top side of trigger, under each grip and on frame under grip.

Those observed by the author have barrel lengths 3", 5½" and 6", with calibers .34 and .36, no engraving.

The single trigger operates both hammers, the right one falling first with slight trigger pull. The left one falling with further trigger pull.

The bag type grips are of walnut and were originally varnished.

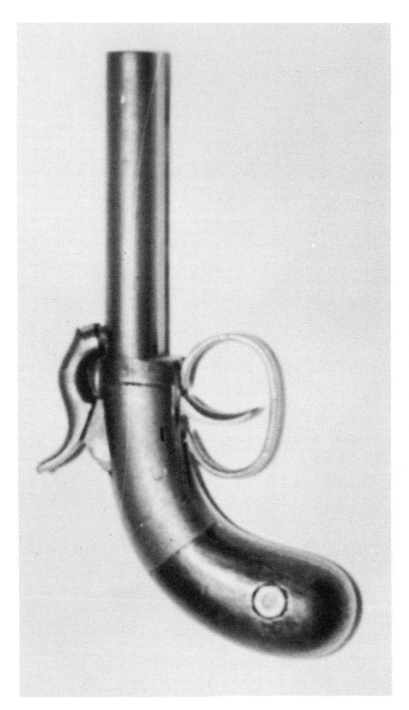

PLATE XI

ALLEN & WHEELOCK, DOUBLE ACTION, SINGLE TRIGGER PISTOL

Markings:
On top flute between barrels: ALLEN & WHEELOCK
Distinctive features: Single trigger

Caliber: .36
Barrel: 3″
Number of shots: 2
Grips: Walnut
Serial number: 544
Finish: Blued

41

Chapter 7

Side Hammer Percussion Revolvers

This chapter will deal with the most interesting model of the Allen & Wheelock production These revolvers were patented in 1857-58 and were manufactured prior to, during, and after the Civil War. There are probably more sizes and variations of this model than any other model manufactured by Allen & Wheelock. They range in size from the large .36 caliber 8″ barrel, Navy Model down to the small .28 caliber 2³/₄″ barrel pocket model.

There are two distinct models. The first model has a different type latch on the combination trigger guard and loading lever, instead of the spring loaded catch on the more common models The trigger guard and spur have a sort of mortised arrangement with enough tension to hold the trigger guard in place.

Also the first model bears different markings from the second model, the Allen & Wheelock name is located on the top flat of barrel instead of on the side, and too the inspection plate on the first model extends down and forms one side of the rear portion of trigger guard.

The following features are common to the first and second model. These single action revolvers have a circular rotating plate with lug, grooved into the rear portion of cylinder for indexing.

They have various sizes of German silver sights mortised into the octagon barrel and a groove in the top strap for the rear sight. The cylinder pin enteres the rear portion of frame, extends through cylinder and front portion of frame acts as bearing for front end of pin. The rear section of pin is threaded into frame.

You will notice that No. 1 of Plate No. XIV is engraved. Although an engraved Allen and Wheelock is seldom found, the master engraver L. D. Nimschke indicated he did extensive work for this firm, as there are four pages of engravings for Allen and Wheelock firearms (mainly rifles) found in L. D. Nimschke's scrapbook recently published by John J. Malloy.

From the author's collection

PLATE XII

Fig. 1
SIDE HAMMER PERCUSSION REVOLVERS
NAVY MODEL

Markings:
ALLEN & WHEELOCK, WORCESTER, MASS. U.S.
Allen's Patents Jan. 13, Dec. 15, 1857, Sept. 7, 1858
On left side of barrel: deep cut cylinder engraving forest scene with rabbit, three buck deers and two does.

Caliber: .36
Barrel: 8"
Number of shots: 6
Grips: Walnut, varnished
Serial number: 555
Finish: Blued barrel, cylinder and frame, casehardened hammer and trigger guard

Fig. 2
POCKET MODEL

Markings:
On top of barrel: ALLEN & WHEELOCK
On side of barrel: Allen's patent Jan. 13, 1857
Distinctive features: Those of the 1st model deep cut cylinder engraving, forest scene with animals

Caliber: .31
Barrel: 6"
Number of shots: 5
Grips: Walnut, varnished
Serial number: 6
Finish: Blued barrel, cylinder and frame, casehardened hammer and trigger guard

Fig. 3
POCKET MODEL

Markings:
ALLEN & WHEELOCK, WORCESTER, MASS. U.S.
Allen's patents Jan. 13, Dec. 15, 1857, Sept. 7, 1858
Deep cut cylinder engraving, forest scene and animals

Caliber: .34
Barrel: 5¾"
Number of shots: 5
Grips: Walnut, varnished
Serial number: 84
Finish: Blued barrel, cylinder and frame, casehardened hammer and trigger guard

Fig. 4
POCKET MODEL

Markings:
ALLEN & WHEELOCK, WORCESTER, MASS. U.S.
Allen's Patents Jan. 13, Dec. 15, 1857, Sept. 7, 1858
Deep cut cylinder engraving, forest scene wth animals

Caliber: .28
Barrel: 2¼"
Number of shots: 5
Grips: Walnut, varnished
Serial number: 346
Finish: Blued barrel, cylinder and frame, casehardened hammer and trigger guard

Fig. 5
POCKET MODEL

Markings:
On left side of barrel: ALLEN & WHEELOCK
WORCESTER, MASS. U.S.
Allen's Patents Jan. 13, Dec. 15, 1857, Sept. 7, 1858
Deep cut cylinder engraving forest scene with animals

Caliber: .34
Barrel: 4⅝"
Number of shots: 5
Grips: Walnut, varnished
Serial number: 537
Finish: Blued barrel, cylinder and frame, casehardened hammer and trigger guard

Fig. 6
POCKET MODEL

Markings:
On left side of barrel: ALLEN & WHEELOCK
WORCESTER, MASS. U.S.
Allen's Patents Jan. 13, Dec. 15, 1857, Sept. 7, 1858
Deep cut cylinder engraving forest scene with animals

Caliber: .34
Barrel: 4"
Number of shots: 5
Grips: Walnut, varnished
Serial number: 301
Finish: Blued barrel, cylinder and frame, casehardened hammer and trigger guard

Fig. 7
POCKET MODEL

Markinsg:
On left side of barrel: ALLEN & WEEHLOCK
WORCESTER, MASS. U.S.
Allen's Patents Jan. 13, Dec. 15, 1857, Sept. 7, 1858
Deep cut cylinder engraving forest scene with animals

Caliber: .28
Barrel: 4"
Number of shots: 5
Grips: Walnut
Serial number: 469
Finish: Blued barrel, cylinder and frame, casehardened hammer and trigger guard

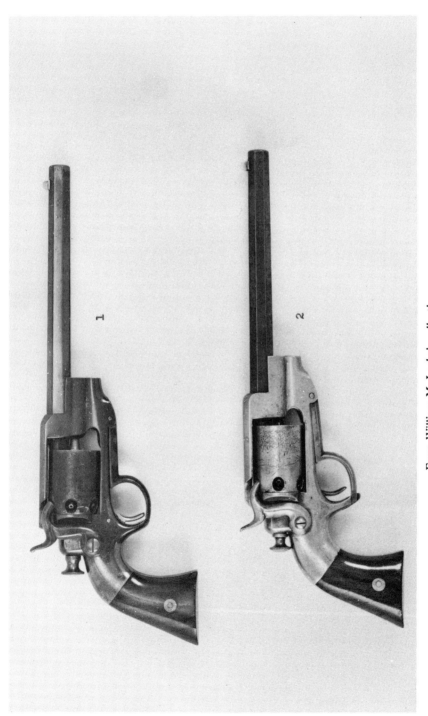

From William M. Locke's collection

48

PLATE XIII

Fig. 1

SIDE HAMMER PERCUSSION REVOLVERS
NAVY MODEL

Markings:
On top of barrel: ALLEN & WHEELOCK
On flat between top and side: Allen's Patent Jan. 13, 1857
Deep cut cylinder engraving
Forest scene with animals
Distinctive features: 1st model, latch, side plate and markings

Fig. 2
NAVY MODEL

Markings:
On left side of barrel: ALLEN & WHEELOCK
WORCESTER, MASS. U.S.
Allen's Patents Jan. 13, Dec. 15, 1857, Sept, 7, 1858
Deep cut cylinder engraving
Forest scene with animals

Caliber: .36
Barrel: $8\frac{5}{16}''$
Number of shots: 6
Grips: Walnut, varnished
Serial number: 13
Finish: Blued barrel, cylinder and frame, casehardened
hammer and trigger guard

Caliber: .36
Barrel: $7\frac{7}{8}''$
Number of shots: 6
Grips: Walnut, varnished
Serial number: 438
Finish: Blued barrel, cylinder and frame, casehardened
hammer and trigger guard

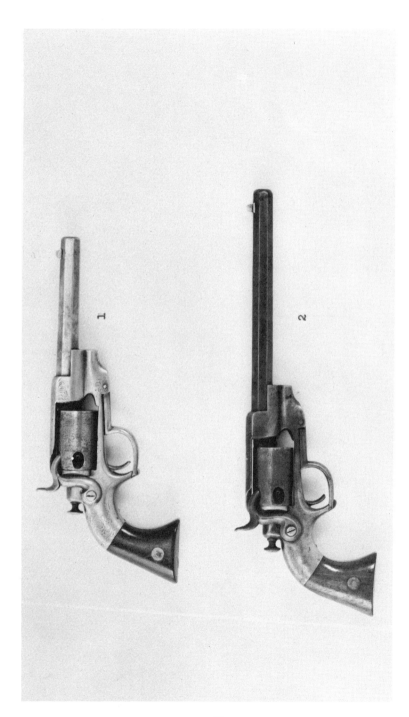

From William M. Locke's collection

PLATE XIV

Fig. 1

SIDE HAMMER PERCUSSION REVOLVERS
POCKET MODEL

Caliber: .31
Barrel: 5″
Number of shots: 5
Grips: Walnut, varnished
Serial number: 93
Finish: Blued cylinder, barrel and frame, casehardened
   hammer and trigger guard

Markings:
   ALLEN & WHEELOCK, WORCESTER, MASS. U.S.
   Allen's Patents Jan. 13, Dec. 15, 1857, Sept. 7, 1858
   Deep cut cylinder engraving
   Distinctive features: Engraved frame

Fig. 2

POCKET MODEL

Caliber: .31
Barrel: 7 7/16″
Number of shots: 6
Grips: Walnut, varnished
Serial number: 386
Finish: Blued barrel, cylinder and frame, casehardened
   hammer and trigger guard

Markings:
   ALLEN & WHEELOCK, WORCESTER, MASS. U.S.
   Allen's Patents Jan. 13, Dec. 15, 1857, Sept. 7, 1858
   Deep cut cylinder engraving
   Forest scene with animals

51

From the author's collection

PLATE XV

SIDE HAMMER PERCUSSION REVOLVER
POCKET MODEL

Caliber: .28
Barrel: 2⅞"
Number of shots: 5
Grips: Walnut, varnished
Serial number: 620
Finish: Blued barrel, cylinder and frame, casehardened hammer and trigger guard

Markings:
  On left side of barrel: ALLEN & WHEELOCK
  WORCESTER, MASS. U.S.
  Allen's Patents Jan. 13, Dec. 15, 1857, Sept. 7, 1858
  Deep cut cylinder engraving, forest scene with animals
  Distinctive features: Cased with accessories

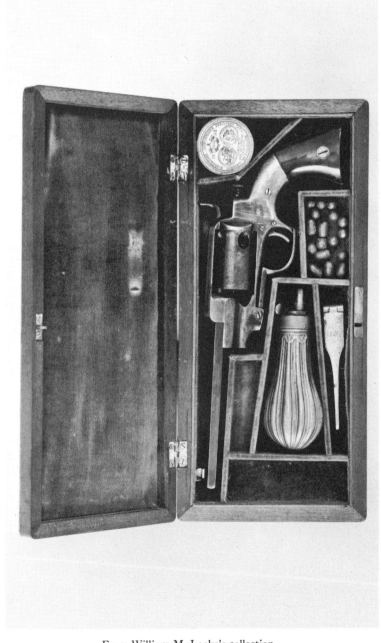

From William M. Locke's collection

PLATE XVI
SIDE HAMMER PERCUSSION REVOLVER
POCKET MODEL

Caliber: .31
Barrel: 5$\frac{13}{16}$"
Number of shots: 5
Grips: Walnut, varnished
Serial number: 25
Finish: Blued barrel, cylinder and frame, casehardened hammer and trigger guard

Markings:
  On left side of barrel: ALLEN & WHEELOCK
  WORCESTER, MASS. U.S.
  Allen's Patents Jan. 13, Dec. 15 1857, Sept. 7, 1858
Deep cut cylinder engraving, forest scene with animals
Distinctive features: Cased with accessories

Chapter 8

Allen & Wheelock Center Hammer
Percussion Revolvers

In this chapter we find a gun that a man could and did go to war with. This ruggedly constructed weapon could match its merits with the best of them during the period of its manufacture.

This model is an easy favorite of the author, as for sturdiness and balance. It would gain recognition with the best of the gun-slingers and soldiers of the eighteen-sixties and seventies.

The U.S. Ordnance purchased about 500 of the big .44 army and navy model and probably would have repeated it many times had not President Lincoln sent a buyer to the European continent about that time, and he placed several orders for guns of similar design.

This gun is truly a handsome proportionate weapon, has brass front sight concaved each side and mortised into barrel, v-notch on lip of center hammer serves as rear sight. The cylinder may be removed, by pressing spring catch at front of frame and removing cylinder pin to front. Walnut grips, blued barrel cylinder and frame, hammer and trigger guard are case hardened in mottled colors. Trigger guard serves as rammer lever when dropped by pressing spring catch at bottom of trigger guard.

The .44 caliber of this model was advertised by Allen & Wheelock as the improved army pistol and stated further that it was unsurpassed for simplicity, strength, power of penetration, and accuracy of shooting. The $^{44}/_{100}$ bore was suited for 28 long or 48 round balls per pound.

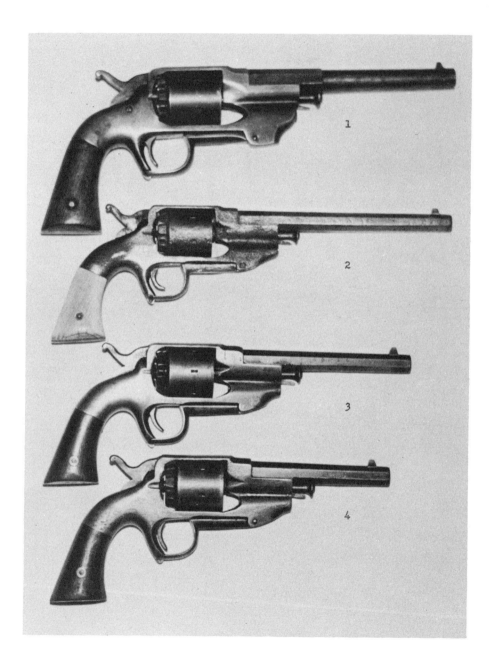

From the author's collection

PLATE XVII

Fig. 1
CENTER HAMMER ARMY MODEL

Caliber: .44
Barrel: 7½" octagon and round
Number of shots: 6
Grips: Walnut, varnished
Serial number: 140
Finish: Blued barrel, cylinder and frame, casehardened hammer and trigger guard

Markings:
On left side of barrel: ALLEN & WHEELOCK WORCESTER, MASS. U.S. Allen's Patents Jan. 13, Dec. 15, 1857, Sept. 7, 1858
Total length: 13¼"
Weight: 2 lbs. 14 oz.
Distinctive feature: cylinder lacking slots near center of cylinder

Fig. 2
CENTER HAMMER NAVY MODEL

Caliber: .36
Barrel: 7½" octagon
Number of shots: 6
Grips: Ivory
Serial number: not visible
Finish: Blued barrel, cylinder and frame, casehardened hammer and trigger guard

Markings:
On left side of barrel: ALLEN & WHEELOCK WORCESTER, MASS. U.S. Allen's Patents Jan. 13, Dec. 15, 1857, Sept. 7, 1858

Fig. 3
CENTER HAMMER POCKET NAVY MODEL

Caliber: .36
Barrel: 6" octagon
Number of shots: 6
Grips: Walnut, varnished
Serial number: 256 on all major parts
Finish: Blued barrel, cylinder and frame, casehardened hammer and trigger guard

Markings:
On left side of barrel: ALLEN & WHEELOCK WORCESTER, MASS. U.S. Allen's Patents Jan. 13, Dec. 15, 1857, Sept. 7, 1858

Fig. 4
CENTER HAMMER POCKET NAVY MODEL

Caliber: .36
Barrel: 5" octagon
Number of shots: 6
Grips: Walnut, varnished
Finish: Blued barrel, cylinder and frame, casehardened hammer and trigger guard

Markings:
On left side of barrel: ALLEN & WHEELOCK WORCESTER, MASS. U.S. Allen's Patents Jan. 13, Dec. 15, 1857, Sept. 7, 1858

Chapter 9

Allen & Wheelock Side Hammer Lipfire Revolvers

The lipfire, a rear-loading variation of the rimfire, was developed by Allen & Wheelock in 1860.

Already rimfire revolvers were in production by a competitive firm, named Smith & Wesson, who controlled the patent rights known as Rollen White patent, which covered the rear loading cylinder using metallic cartridges.

Having secured the patent rights for the lipfire cartridge in 1860, Allen & Wheelock started manufacturing pistols to use the lipfire cartridge, but in 1863, Smith & Wesson secured an injunction which forced Allen & Wheelock to suspend all production of revolving arms, with chambers bored through for loading at the rear.

However, from the period between 1860 and 1863 Allen & Wheelock brought out some very interesting revolvers with ejecting mechanisms that would stagger the imagination. The principle difference between these revolvers and the regular rimfire was the cylinder having a slot at each chamber to accommodate the lip of the cartridge as the whole cartridge rested within the cylinder with only the protruding lip extending up in the slot where it could be struck by the hammer.

The side hammer revolvers were equipped with a loading gate on the left side that was held in a closed position by a rachet type lever that also actuated the ejector which was built into an integral part of the steel frame.

This model was equipped with a spur trigger, octagon barrel, front cylinder pin released by a spring loaded pin under the frame, the front sight was a large brass blade type with wide base and concave side mortised into top of barrel. The top strap was grooved for the rear sight.

It was .32 caliber using the Allen & Wheelock No. 52 lipfire cartridge, barrel lengths observed by the author were 4″, 5″ and 6″ long.

The patent attorneys advised Mr. Wesson of Smith & Wesson that they had an airtight case against the firm of Allen & Wheelock for infringement on the Rollen White patent by producing a bored through cylinder. Mr. Wesson expressed regrets about going after these fellows. He said "My partner and I worked for years for Allen & Wheelock." He suggested that instead of prosecuting, they write to them and suggest that they stop producing them of their own accord. "If they won't, we will sue them along with the rest." (There were many infringements upon their patent at that time.)

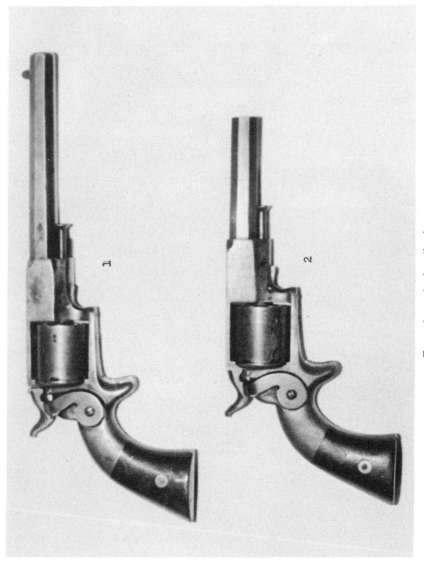

PLATE XVIII

ALLEN & WHEELOCK SIDE HAMMER, LIPFIRE REVOLVERS

Fig. 1

Caliber: .32 or No. 52 Allen lipfire
Barrel: 6″
Number of shots: 6
Grips: Walnut, varnished
Serial number: 11
Finish: Blued frame, cylinder and barrel, casehardened hammer

Markings:
On left side of barrel: ALLEN & WHEELOCK
WORCESTER, MASS. U.S.
Allen's Patents Sept. 7, Nov. 9, 1858, July 3, 1860

Fig. 2

Caliber: .32 or No. 52 Allen lipfire
Barrel: 4″
Number of shots: 6
Grips: Walnut, varnished
Serial number: 296
Finish: Blued frame, barrel and cylinder, casehardened hammer

Markings:
On left side of barrel: ALLEN & WHEELOCK
WORCESTER, MASS. U.S.
Allen's Patent Sept. 7, Nov. 9, 1858, July 3, 1860
Distinctive feature: barrel has been shortened

63

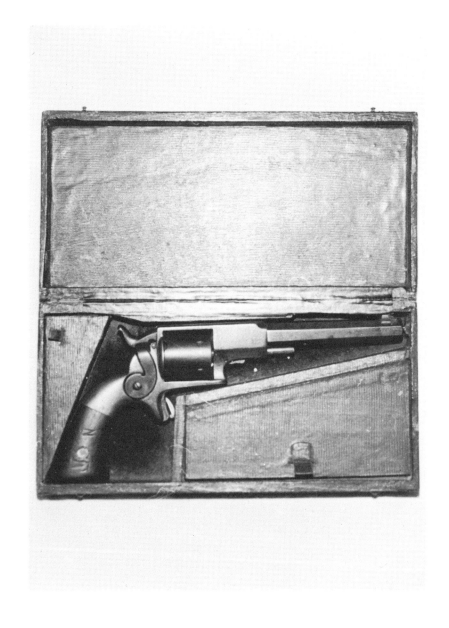

From the author's collection

PLATE XIX

ALLEN & WHEELOCK SIDE HAMMER LIPFIRE REVOLVER

Caliber: .32 or No. 52 Allen Lipfire
Barrel: 5″
Number of shots: 6
Grips: Walnut, varnished
Serial number: 99
Finish: Blued barrel, cylinder and frame, casehardened hammer

Markings:
On left side of barrel: ALLEN & WHEELOCK WORCESTER, MASS. U.S. Allen's Patents Sept. 7, Nov. 9, 1858, July 3, 1860
Distinctive features: Cased in black leatherette covered wood case with red leatherette lining

Chapter 10

Center Hammer Lipfire Revolvers

All gun enthusiasts have marveled at the determination of the inventors of this model to maintain the same appearance of the trigger guard, as on previous models, while at the same time using it for a different purpose. Allen & Wheelock characteristicly used the trigger guard for a loading lever with great success; they also needed an ejector to operate on the side of the frame and by the most ingenious arrangement they accomplished the task. My vocabulary will not adequately describe it, will advise you to examine this mechanism.

This model was produced in two calibers .36 or No. 56 Allen lipfire and .44 or No. 58 Allen lipfire. The first, called the navy model, has an octagon barrel and the latter called the army model, has the part octagon and part round barrel with the usual brass front sight and a raised portion of frame in front of hammer, v-notched for rear sight. The loading gates are located on the right side; some are hinged at the top and some are hinged at the bottom, with a spring catch to hold them in place. Also the grips have a greater flare at the base on some models.

It cannot easily be established how many of these guns were produced, however in the opinion of the writer any model or variation of the lipfire revolver is much scarcer than the eagerly sought after Colt Patterson or Colt Walker pistols.

This model was a handsome, sturdy, well balanced, practical firearm of its day and will probably be forever cherished by the collector.

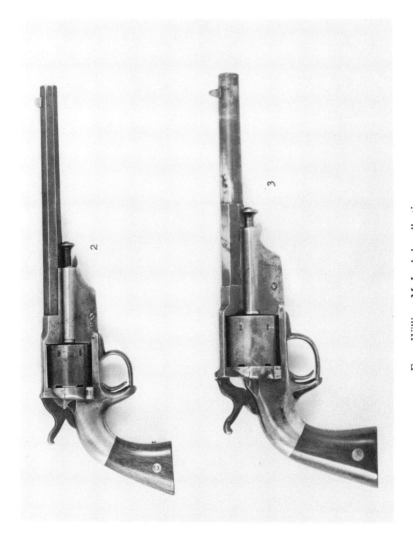

PLATE XX

ALLEN & WHEELOCK CENTER HAMMER LIPFIRE REVOLVER

Fig. 2

Markings:
ALLEN & WHEELOCK
WORCESTER, MASS. U.S.
Allen's Patents Sept. 7, Nov. 9, 1858

Caliber: .38 or No. 56 Allen lipfire
Barrel: 8"
Number of shots: 6
Grips: Walnut, varnished
Serial number: 416
Finish: Blued barrel, cylinder and frame,
casehardened hammer

Fig. 3

Markings:
ALLEN & WHEELOCK
WORCESTER, MASS. U.S.
Allen's Patents Sept. 7, Nov. 9, 1858

Caliber: .44 or No. 58 Allen lipfire
Barrel: 7½"
Number of shots: 6
Grips: Walnut, varnished
Serial number: 00
Finish: Blued barrel, cylinder and frame,
casehardened trigger

PLATE XXI

ALLEN & WHEELOCK CENTER HAMMER LIPFIRE REVOLVER

Fig. 1

Markings:
On left side of barrel: ALLEN & WHEELOCK
WORCESTER, MASS. U.S.
Allen's Patents Sept. 7, Nov. 9, 1858

Fig. 2

Markings:
On left side of barrel: ALLEN & WHEELOCK
WORCESTER, MASS. U.S.
Allen's Patents Sept 7, Nov. 9, 1858
Distinctive feature: Flaw in casting on ejector housing

Caliber: .38 or No. 56 Allen lipfire
Barrel: 6" long
Number of shots: 6
Grips: Walnut, varnished
Serial number: 319
Finish: Blued barrel, cylinder and frame,
casehardened hammer

Caliber: .38 or No. 56 Allen lipfire
Barrel: 5" long
Number of shots: 6
Grips: Walnut, varnished
Serial number: .22
Finish: Blued barrel, cylinder and frame,
casehardened hammer

Chapter 11

Allen & Wheelock Center Hammer Conversion Revolvers

Surely after reading the "Rebuttal to an Unusual Allen & Wheelock" by Philip F. Van Cleave, in the May 1960, issue of the *Gun Report* all collectors will agree that the center hammer Allen & Wheelock rimfire revolvers are conversions and those observed by the writer were converted from the lipfire model. Surely no firearm could be converted to use the rimfire cartridge as easily as this one.

The .44 lipfire was changed to use the .44 Henry rimfire cartridge. The .36 caliber was changed to use the .38 rimfire cartridge; it is most likely that all these conversions were the work of private gunsmiths, long after they left the factory.

These conversions were produced simply by machining away chamber walls down even with the bottom of the slots provided for lips of the former cartridges and by enlarging the loading groove through recoil shield and frame to allow for the larger rim on the rimfire cartridge.

The discriminating collector will discover three variations of this model Allen & Wheelock. The first being the hinged loading gate, some are fastened at the top, some are fastened at the bottom. Second, the flare at the base of the grips are wider on some than on others. On the third variation the serial numbers are placed on the rear end of the cylinder while on the two previous variations they were stamped on the forward end of the cylinder.

The .38 caliber revolvers have octagon barrels, slightly tapered toward the muzzle. The .44 caliber has the typical, part octagon, part round barrel.

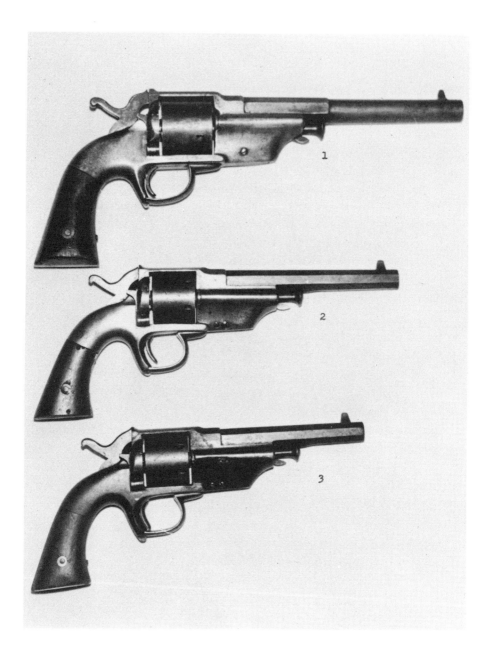

From the author's collection

PLATE XXII

RIM FIRE CONVERSION

Fig. 1

Caliber: .44
Barrel: 7½"
Number of shots: 6
Grips: Walnut, varnished
Serial number: 157
Finish: Blued frame, barrel and cylinder, casehardened hammer

Markings:
On left side of barrel: ALLEN & WHEELOCK WORCESTER, MASS. U.S. Allen's Patents Sept. 7, Nov. 9, 1858

Fig. 2

Caliber: .38
Barrel: 6"
Number of shots: 6
Grips: Walnut, varnished
Serial number: 156
Finish: Blued frame, barrel and cylinder, casehardened trigger

Markings:
On left side of barrel: ALLEN & WHEELOCK WORCESTER, MASS. U.S. Allen's Patents Sept. 7, Nov. 9, 1858

Fig. 3

Caliber: .38
Barrel: 5"
Number of shots: 6
Grips: Walnut, varnished
Serial number: 201
Finish: Blued barrel, frame and cylinder, casehardened trigger

Markings:
On left side of barrel: ALLEN & WHEELOCK WORCESTER, MASS. U.S. Allen's Patents Sept. 7, Nov. 9, 1858

Chapter 12

Center Hammer Single Shot Rimfire Pistols

Here is further evidence that the inventors Allen & Wheelock tried everything and would stop at nothing to meet all manner of competition.

To the collector of today who would enjoy a real challenge and at the same time specialize with one manufacturers product, the numerous models and varieties of the Allen & Wheelock would keep him interested and searching for many years and it would be doubtful that he would be able to find them all, especially at sensible prices. He would be amazed at the low serial numbers. The writer knows one collector who is trying to see how many he can collect with consecutive serial numbers. Another collector in Cleveland, Ohio, has informed the writer that he has serial No. 1 of the big lipfire army model. The large side hammer 8″ barrel navy model in near mint condition was sold for $1,200.00 at the 1960 annual Gun Report show at Dodge City, Kansas, so you can see that the word is out as to the scarcity of these guns.

The pistols mentioned at the heading of this chapter are indeed a scarce item. You will attend many collectors meetings without seeing a single speciman. They have an octagon barrel that is squared up at the breech. By placing the hammer at half cock you are able to swing the breech to the right for loading or ejecting, by a very clever device that is actuated by an attachment on the end of the frame which when moved to the left causes the ejector to slide out a groove in bottom of barrel. Has the bead type front sight and a v-slot rear sight mortised in top of barrel, also has top of frame slotted to further assist in lining up the sights, hammer and trigger screw enter from the left side. There is no inspection plate and the barrel is secured by a screw in the bottom of the frame. The serial number is located on each grip frame and under barrel.

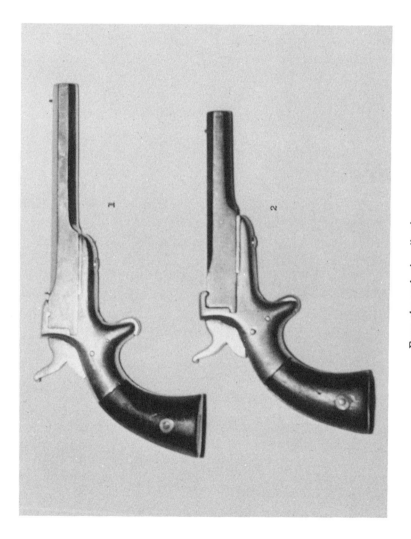

PLATE XXIII

Fig. 1

CENTER HAMMER, SINGLE SHOT, RIMFIRE PISTOL

Markings:
  On side of barrel: ALLEN & WHEELOCK
    WORCESTER, MASS.
  Distinctive feature: Absence of any patent dates

Fig. 2

Markings:
  On side of barrel: ALLEN & WHEELOCK
    WORCESTER, MASS.
  Distinctive feature: Absence of any patent dates

Caliber: .32
Barrel: 5"
Number of shots: 1
Grips: Walnut, varnished
Serial number: 511
Finish: Nickel plate

Caliber: .32
Barrel: 4"
Number of shots: 1
Grips: Walnut, varnished
Serial number: 564
Finish: Blued

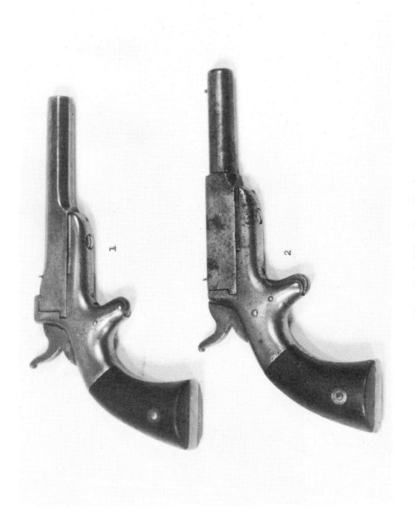

From Jack Wilson's collection

PLATE XXIV

CENTER HAMMER, SINGLE SHOT, RIMFIRE PISTOLS

Fig. 1

Markings:
On left side of barrel: ALLEN & WHEELOCK
WORCESTER, MASS.
Distinctive feature: Absence of any patent dates

Caliber: .32 rimfire
Barrel: 4½"
Number of shots: 1
Grips: Walnut, varnished
Serial number: 542
Finish: Blued

Fig. 2

Markings:
On left side of barrel: ALLEN & WHEELOCK
WORCESTER, MASS.
Distinctive feature: Part round barrel and absence of any
patent dates

Caliber: .32 rimfire
Barrel: 4½"
Number of shots: 1
Grips: Walnut, varnished
Serial number: 888
Finish: Blued

81

Chapter 13

Allen & Wheelock Side Hammer Rimfire Revolvers

Rimfire revolvers were produced with both steel and brass frames, the brass frames being very difficult to locate or obtain, they are identical to the steel frame in all respects.

The collector will find better picking with this model than any of the others, but don't expect people to come knocking on your door with them. However, there are enough variations of this model to keep the collector busy for some time. The only things common to all models are the octagon barrels and side hammers. They come in a variety of calibers and barrel lengths. The cylinder pin is inserted from the front with a spring lever catch on some models, on others the pin enters at the rear of the frame and held in place with a small spring loaded pin mounted in bottom of recoil shield. This is found on the small .22 calibers, also on some models there is a screw with a knurled head inserted in the bottom of the frame in front of the spur trigger which holds the cylinder pin in place.

Some of the larger calibers have deep cut engraving depicting a forest scene, with house, rail fence, hunter with gun, three dogs, three rabbits and a man holding a horse saddled and bridled. The little shot .22 caliber has five different scenes in circular panels. The first has the great seal of Massachusetts, the second crossed rifles, two pistols, a bar hammer single shot, a side hammer revolver and hunting pouch. The third a stand of arms, drum, sword, halberd, pipes, bayonets, cannons, barrel, dirk and flags. The fourth, a mounted spearman on charging horse, the fifth, a sailing vessel passing fort, while others have no cylinder engraving. All are equipped with front sights and groove in the top of the frame for the rear sight.

Located in the section of History and Technology at the Smithsonian Institution, Washington D.C., there is a glass enclosed booth containing some of the personal belongings of Abraham Lincoln, among these is displayed the Allen and Wheelock shown on plate XXVII-B. This revolver was presented by Lincoln's great grandson Lincoln Isham.

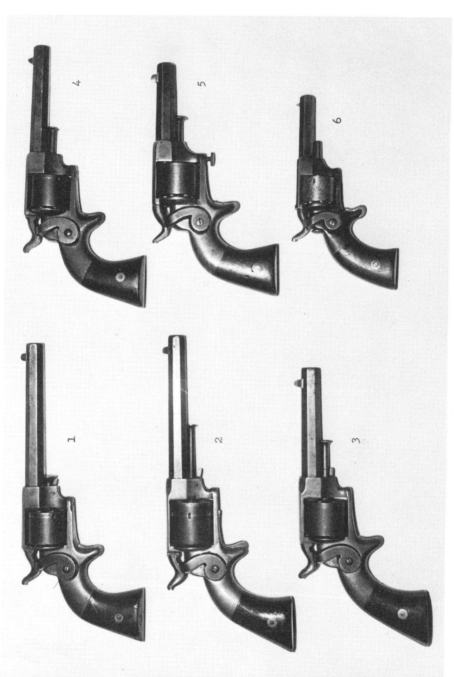

From the author's collection

PLATE XXV

Fig. 1

THE SIDE HAMMER RIM FIRE REVOLVER

Markings:
On left side of barrel: ALLEN & WHEELOCK
WORCESTER, MASS. U.S.
Allen's Patents Sept. 7, Nov. 9, 1858
On left side of frame: July 3, 1860

Caliber: .32 short
Barrel: 5"
Number of shots: 6
Grips: Walnut, varnished
Serial number: 119
Finish: Blued
Cylinder length: $1\frac{15}{16}''$

Fig. 2

Markings:
On left side of barrel: ALLEN & WHEELOCK
WORCESTER, MASS. U.S.
Allen's Patents Sept. 7, Nov. 9, 1858
On left side of frame: July 3, 1860
Distinctive feature: Brass frame

Caliber: .32 long
Barrel: $4\frac{7}{8}''$
Number of shots: 6
Grips: Walnut, varnished
Serial number: 206
Finish: Blued barrel and cylinder
Cylinder length: $1\frac{3}{16}''$

Fig. 3

Markings:
On left side of barrel: ALLEN & WHEELOCK
WORCESTER, MASS. U.S.
Allen's Patents Sept. 7, Nov. 9, 1858
On left side of frame: July 3, 1860
Distinctive feature: Brass frame

Caliber: .32 short
Barrel: $3\frac{7}{8}''$
Number of shots: 6
Grips: Walnut, varnished
Serial number: 71
Finish: Blued barrel and cylinder
Cylinder length: $\frac{15}{16}''$

Fig. 4

Markings:
On left side of barrel: ALLEN & WHEELOCK
WORCESTER, MASS. U.S.
Allen's Patents Sept. 7, Nov. 9, 1858
On left side of frame: July 3, 1860

Caliber: .32 short
Barrel: 4"
Number of shots: 6
Grips: Walnut, varnished
Serial number: 1451
Finish: Blued
Cylinder length: $\frac{15}{16}''$

Fig. 5

Markings:
On left side of barrel: ALLEN & WHEELOCK
WORCESTER, MASS. U.S.
Allen's Patents Sept. 7, Nov. 9, 1858
On left side of frame: July 3, 1860

Caliber: .32 short
Barrel: 3"
Number of shots: 6
Grips: Walnut, varnished
Serial number: 317
Finish: Blued
Cylinder length: $\frac{15}{16}''$

Fig. 6

Markings:
On left side of barrel: ALLEN & WHEELOCK
WORCESTER, MASS. U.S.
Allen's Patents Sept. 7, Nov. 9, 1858
On left side of frame: July 3, 1860

Caliber: .22 short
Barrel: $2\frac{3}{8}''$
Number of shots: 7
Grips: Walnut, varnished
Serial number: 62
Finish: Blued
Cylinder length: $\frac{23}{32}''$

PLATE XXVI

SIDE HAMMER RIMFIRE REVOLVER

Caliber: .32 rimfire
Barrel: 3¾"
Number of shots: 6
Grips: Walnut, varnished
Serial number: 838
Finish: Blued

Markings:
On left side of barrel: ALLEN & WHEELOCK
WORCESTER, MASS. U.S.
Allen's Patents Sept. 7, Nov. 9, 1858
Distinctive feature: Engraved

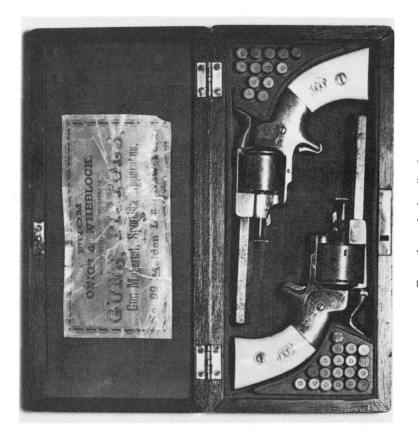

From the author's collection

PLATE XXVII

SIDE HAMMER RIMFIRE REVOLVER

TOP

Markings:
On left side of barrel: ALLEN & WHEELOCK
WORCESTER, MASS. U.S.
Allen's Patents Sept. 7, Nov. 9, 1858
Distinctive features: Ivory grips and double cased

Caliber: .22
Barrel: $2\frac{15}{16}$" long
Number of shots: 7
Grips: Ivory, monogramed each side
Serial number: 203
Finish: Blued barrel, cylinder and frame,
caseharedened hammer

BOTTOM

Markings:
On left side of barrel: ALLEN & WHEELOCK
WORCESTER, MASS. U.S.
Allen's Patents Sept. 7, Nov. 9, 1858
Distinctive features: Ivory grips, double cased

Caliber: .22
Barrel: $2\frac{15}{16}$" long
Number of shots: 7
Grips: Ivory, monogramed each side
Serial number: 197
Finish: Blued barrel, cylinder and frame,
caseharedened hammer

91

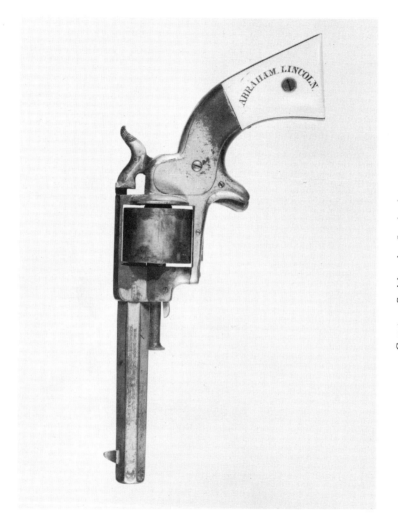

PLATE XXVII-B

SIDE HAMMER RIM FIRE REVOLVER

LINCOLN GUN

Markings:
On left side of barrel: ALLEN & WHEELOCK
WORCESTER, MASS. U.S.
Allen's Patents Sept. 7, Nov. 9, 1858
On right side of frame: July 9, 1860
Distinctive features: Ivory grips with Abraham Lincoln
engraved on left grip

Caliber: .31
Barrel: 3⅞″
Number of shots: 6
Grips: Ivory
Serial number: 439
Finish: Tin Plated

Chapter 14

Allen & Wheelock Cartridges

A very important phase of the Allen & Wheelock operation was the metallic cartridge. At this time, metallic cartridge making was a very tedious and slow hand process. Allen & Wheelock made and patented the first machine for doing this job.

It caused reverberations around the world. Those who were interested in such patents saw that this system would revolutionize cartridge manufacturing, so they went to work with their legal eagles, but they were driven off.

This firm exhibited its invention at the Centennial Exposition of 1876 and one observer wrote that "nothing in the mechanical line attracted more attention" than Allen's astounding invention.

The Worcester firearms pioneer had hit pay dirt at that period in arms making, when the loading of firearms was being changed from muzzle-loading to breech-loading. Instead of buying balls, powder and caps, the users were able to purchase ammunition already fixed and boxed, and in essentially the same form that we use today.

On September 25, 1860, the Allen & Wheelock firm obtained patent number 30,109 for the lipfire cartridge, which states as follows: "The nature of my invention consists in constructing a lip on a metallic cartridge for the reception of a fulminate.

"By confining the fulminate to the projection or lip, I thereby save about a seven-eights of the expense of this compound and lessen the liability in the same proportion of blowing off the cartridge end which often occurs in common use.

"I also make a stronger head or end to the cartridge, which obviates the difficulty of the swelling back of the head of the cartridge, as is common in other modes of construction."

Allen & Wheelock cartridges were sized as follows:

Caliber .25 was number 50 Allen lipfire
Caliber .32 was number 52 Allen lipfire
Caliber .38 was number 56 Allen lipfire
Caliber .44 was number 58 Allen lipfire

Some Allen & Wheelock cartridges have the A. & W. head stamp. These are much sought after by cartridge collectors. The writer has observed some boxes of pinfire cartridges bearing the Allen label.

A hundred years ago there seemed to be much concern about the safety of self-contained cartridges. It is reported that Mr. Wesson of Smith and Wesson was giving a demonstration on the safety of the rimfire cartridge and he threw one with great force into a fireplace. By a quirk of fate, the rim struck an andiron and the shell exploded, but quickly and in a satisfied manner, Mr. Wesson remarked, "See what great force it took to set it off."

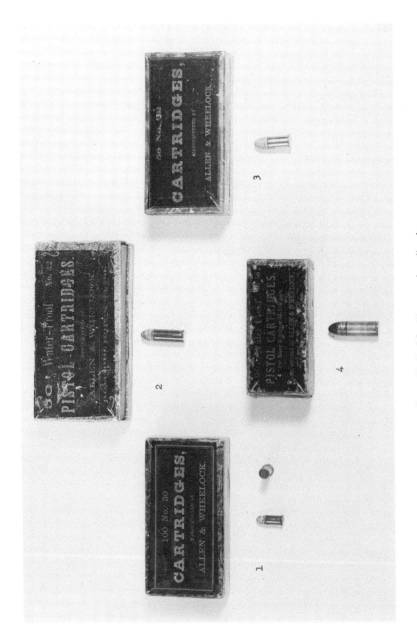

From H. R. Mouillesseaux's collection

96

PLATE XXVIII

ALLEN AND WHEELOCK CARTRIDGES

Fig. 1

50 WATER-PROOF NO. 52
PISTOL CARTRIDGES
MANUFACTURED BY
ALLEN & WHEELOCK
ALLEN'S PATENT SEPTEMBER 25th, 1860

Fig. 4

2 DOZ. WATER-PROOF NO. 56
PISTOL CARTRIDGES
FOR NAVY REVOLVER 36-100 BORE
MANUFACTURED BY ALLEN & WHEELOCK
ALLEN'S PATENT SEPTEMBER 25th, 1860

Chapter 15

Allen & Wheelock
Double Barrel Shotguns

I have wondered just how scarce the Allen & Wheelock shotgun really is. The one pictured in this chapter is the only one the writer has been able to handle.

In 1864 a history of American manufacturers reported the manufacture of revolvers and guns by Allen & Wheelock was quite extensive.

These are so similiar in appearance to the dozens of different manufacture's muzzle loading shotguns that many have been passed by unnoticed.

A book titled *Industrial Worcester* speaks of this company's invention of a double-barrled breech-loading shotgun and further states that it was probably the first to use metallic shells in connection with such a firearm, these shells could be reloaded indefinitely. The article goes on to point out that they were pioneers in this country, in the manufacture of double-barreled shot guns and fowling pieces, and that neither in this country or in Europe had metallic shells been made except by hand.

Another book titled *Massachusetts Industries* states that no man in the world made a greater contribution in improvements and in the invention of machinery in the firearms field than this ingenious mechanic Ethan Allen, and that his firm was among the first to adopt the breech-loading system in place of the muzzle-loading type.

The muzzle-loading shotgun pictured on plate twenty-eight, has very graceful lines for this type gun and has a select piece of walnut with some graceful checkering for the stock. It is equipped with flash guards behind the percussion nipples.

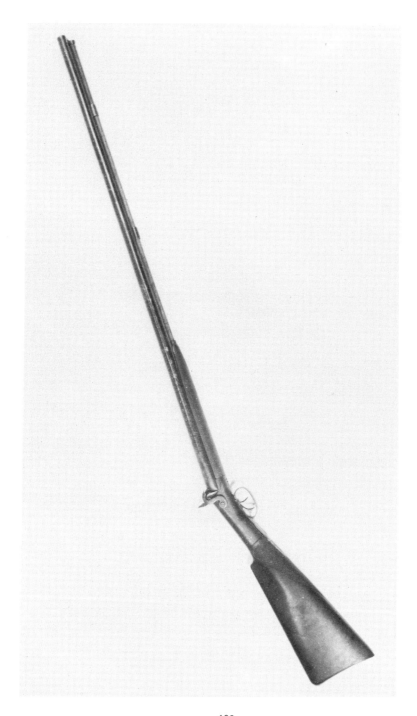

From Jack Wilson's collection

100

PLATE XXIX

ALLEN AND WHEELOCK DOUBLE BARREL SHOTGUN

Gauge: 12
Barrel length: 36¾"
Stock: Walnut, checkered at wrist
Number of shots: 2
Serial number: 2
Finish: Damascus twist barrels

Markings:
  On rib between barrels: ALLEN & WHEELOCK
Distinctive feature: The mechanism is enclosed in steel rounded section forming part of the wrist where it joins the stock

Chapter 16

Allen & Wheelock Single Shot, Percussion Rifles

Here is a rifle whose loading instructions specified that after pouring the powder in the muzzle you pour in a little rock salt ahead of the ball so when shooting game at long range the meat would keep until you could get to it. Actually "the rule of thumb" for the powder measure was to place the ball in the palm of your hand and pour powder on top of ball until it was covered, then you had the correct powder charge.

These rifles were muzzle-loading with rifled barrels which had a blade type front sight and v-notch rear sight mortised into the top of barrel. The barrel is octagon to round approximately one third octagon next to breech, with flash shield an integral part of the lock, single trigger and center set hammer offset to right side to line up with percussion nipple. Has inspection plate on right side of lock, barrel had one forward sleeve and long tube under octagon section to store ramrod, has spur approximately three inches rear of trigger guard and one and three quarter inch tang with screw into bottom of stock. The stock is of walnut with medium concave at butt for shoulder rest. Has iron butt plate with two inch extension over top of butt.

The lock extended back far enough to form the wrist section, which is normally part of the stock on most rifles by other manufacturers.

Who could say how many times such a rifle as this kept meat on the table for the frontier family, or played a part in holding off attacks by savage Indians, or saved a man acting in self defense against a rattlesnake during the great westward move?

One needs to remember that at the time Allen & Wheelock brought out this long rifle they were competing with
the Sharps, Hawken, and dozens of other plains rifle makers
Realizing the determination of the Allen & Wheelock firm to
meet all manner of competition whether it be the Colt
revolving rifle or the suicide special, one can be sure that
this rifle was no inferior weapon even when in the company
of more renown rifle makers.

PLATE XXX

ALLEN & WHEELOCK MUZZLE LOADING, SINGLE SHOT, PERCUSSION RIFLE

Markings:
On top of barrel flat: ALLEN & WHEELOCK

Caliber: .44
Barrel length: 36¾"
Number of shots: 1
Stock: Walnut, varnished
Serial number: 2
Finish: Browned barrel, casehardened lock

105

Chapter 17

Allen & Wheelock Breech-Loading Side Hammer Percussion Rifle

This rifle has at least two aliases — the "faucet breech" and the "tap breech", adopted because the breech was opened and closed by a lever mounted on top of lock resembling the operation of a water faucet or water tap. The patent was granted on July 3, 1855 for this very unique and unusual breech-loading percussion rifle, the top lever with the finger loop rotated the breech for loading paper cartridges and also an access for cleaning the bore.

There appears to have been an earlier and also later models of this rifle. Some of the earlier ones were possibly equipped with circular patch box and six groove rifling, while the latter ones omitted the patchbox and had three groove rifling. They were stocked with high grade walnut, also walnut forends. The barrel was octagon to round with blade type front sight, adjustable rear sight on some specimens, others with various types of sights probably installed after they left the factory.

Possibly less than two hundred of these were produced as all serial numbers so far observed are well under this number.

One cannot help but wonder if the other drop breech rifle that has won such great acclaim did not get some ideas from this sturdy breech of similar design. Had it not made its appearance so near the end of the percussion period it would have been produced in great numbers as it is a very well balanced rifle, and as attractive in appearance as the single shot rifles being manufactured today.

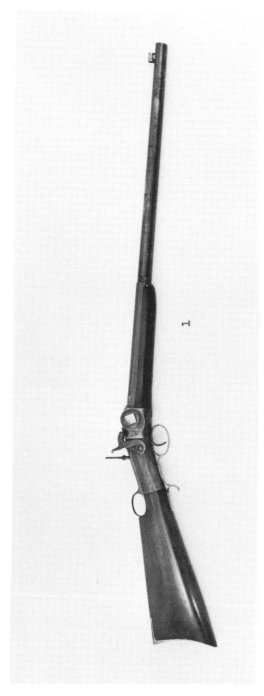

1

From William M. Locke's collection

PLATE XXXI

ALLEN & WHEELOCK BREECH LOADING SIDE HAMMER PERCUSSION RIFLE

Caliber: .42
Barrel length: 27½"
Number of shots: 1
Serial number: 161

Markings:
On top of octagon section of barrel:
ALLEN & WHEELOCK
Allen's patent July 3, 1855
Number manufactured: Estimated less than 200

Chapter 18

Allen & Wheelock Lipfire Revolving Rifles

Although Allen & Wheelock's fame rests largely on the hand guns they produced, they could not resist the revolving system in the manufacture of long guns making them multishot weapons.

However, revolving firearms had been in existance for about three hundred years. A revolving matchlock with manually operated cylinder was manufactured and used in the Orient as early as the seventeenth century. Approximately fifty years before the Allen & Wheelock revolving rifle was patented, Elisha Collier, a Boston gunsmith, had introduced a revolving cylinder rifle and pistol under an English patent.

For some reason the revolving long guns were never popular with the army, therefore very few of them saw any military use. They were laid aside for the single shot muskets. Although popular in the frontier days, revolving shoulder arms are not very familiar to the average individual; they are a very interesting and much sought after weapon by collectors.

The year 1865 was virtually the end of the muzzle loading firearm; caused partly by the inspection of muskets gathered up from the battle of Gettysburg. Some guns were found with two and three loads on top of each other, the soldier in his excitement would forget he had just loaded and would repeat the process, and there was no way to view the loaded chamber. If some of these had been fired they would have killed not only the rifleman, but some of his near-by comrades.

The Allen & Wheelock revolving lipfire rifle pictured on the following plate has a very trim appearance and when handled by a gunman he cannot resist putting it to his shoulder and taking careful aim as if his life depended on hitting the target.   It is stocked with a beautiful piece of curly walnut.

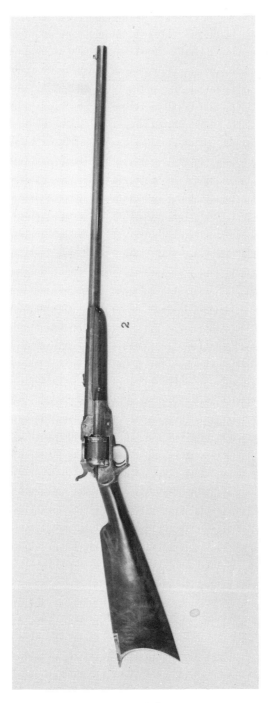

2

From William M. Locke's collection

PLATE XXXII

ALLEN & WHEELOCK LIPFIRE REVOLVING RIFLE

Caliber: .44 or No. 58 Allen lipfire
Barrel length: 27½" octagon to round
Number of shots: 6
Stock & forend: Circassian walnut
Serial number: 161
Finish: Blued barrel, casehardened frame, trigger guard and hammer

Number manufactured: Estimated at less than 200
Distinctive feature: Lack of any patent dates
Sights: German silver front and adjustable step rear sight

113

Chapter 19

Allen & Wheelock Drop Breech Rimfire Rifles

The patent covering this action was issued to E. Allen, September 18, 1860, number 30033. A rimfire rifle, calibers observed by the writer .31, .32, .41, and .44, octagon to round barrels from $23^3/4''$ to $25^7/8''$ long.

Releasing the catch in the rear of the trigger-guard allows the latter to be swung forward, and in so doing ejects the empty shell and opens the breech. The rear sight is equipped with an indicator which swings over an arc graduated from 0-10.

On top of the barrel is stamped, "Allen & Wheelock, Allen's pat Sept. 18, 1860." The stock is fastened to the frame with a screw accessible through springed access door in butt plate.

Some specimens have a metal cap on the walnut forend, some do not, some have carrying sling loops located just forward of the forend attached to the barrel band and on the swivel plate mounted in the bottom of stock. Blade sights of various types are mortised into the muzzle end of barrel. The cartridge rim is struck by a plunger extending through the one and one half inch breech block.

The single shot rifle has been set aside for the most part by shooters in favor of the various types of repeaters, but they still hold a fascination for the collector. They bring back thoughts of the easy slow life before we became plagued with all the tensions of high pressure living.

In the days when the single shot rifle was having its heyday the owner of a good target rifle took great pride in

it and was able to use it for profit. Most of the country
at that time was game country and the single shot rifle
owner could leisurely make the kill with one well placed
shot.

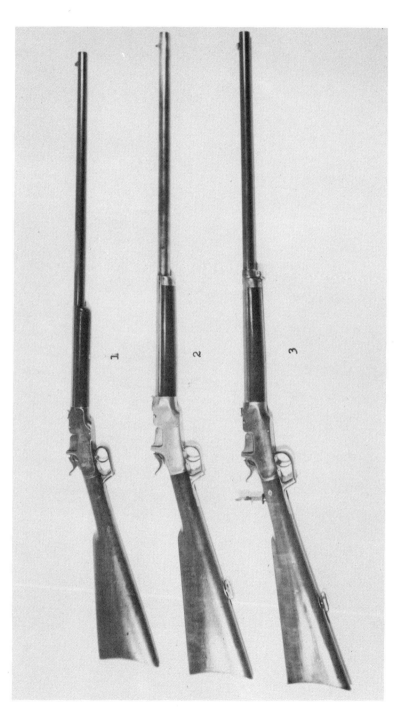

From Jack Wilson's collection

PLATE XXXIII

DROP BREECH SINGLE SHOT RIFLES

Fig. 1

Markings:
On top of barrel: ALLEN & WHEELOCK
Allen's patent Sept. 18, 1860
Distinctive feature: Absence of forend cap or sling loops

Caliber: .32 rimfire
Barrel length: 23¾"
Number of shots: 1
Stock and forend: Walnut
Serial number: 166
Finish: Blued barrel, casehardened frame, hammer and trigger guard

Fig. 2

Markings:
On top of barrel: ALLEN & WHEELOCK
Allen's Patent Sept. 18, 1860
Distinctive feature: sling loops

Caliber: .41 rimfire
Barrel length: 24"
Number of shots: 1
Stock and forend: Walnut
Serial number: 1179
Finish: Blued barrel, casehardened frame, hammer and trigger guard

Fig. 3

Markings:
On top of barrel: ALLEN & WHEELOCK
Allen's Patent Sept. 18, 1860
Distinctive feature: Sling loops

Caliber: .44 rimfire
Barrel length: 24⅞"
Number of shots: 1
Stock and forend: Walnut
Serial number: 1451
Finish: Blued barrel, casehardened frame, hammer and trigger guard

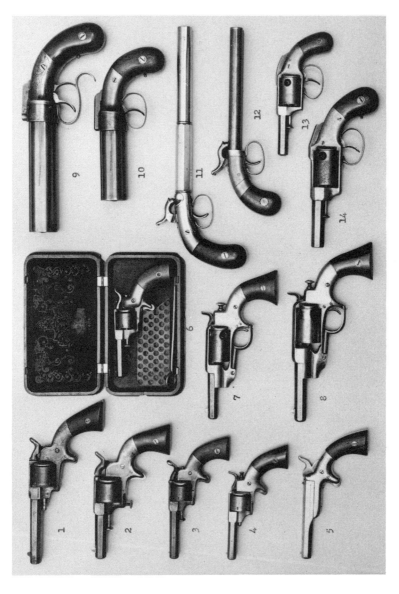

Group of Allen & Wheelocks from the collection of W. B. Sisler, Portland, Oregon.

PLATE XXXIV

Fig. 1

RIMFIRE POCKET REVOLVER

Markings:
On left side of barrel: ALLEN & WHEELOCK
WORCESTER, MASS. U.S.
Allen's Patents Sept. 7, Nov. 9, 1858
On left side of frame: July 3, 1860

Caliber: .30
Barrel length: 4"
Number of shots: 6
Grips: Walnut
Serial number: 511
Finish: Nickle plated

Fig. 2

RIMFIRE POCKET REVOLVER

Markings:
On left side of barrel: ALLEN & WHEELOCK
WORCESTER, MASS. U.S.
Allen's Patents Sept. 7, Nov. 9, 1858
On left side of frame: July 3, 1860

Caliber: .30
Barrel length: 3"
Number of shots: 6
Grips: Walnut
Serial number: 78
Finish: Blued

Fig. 3

RIMFIRE POCKET REVOLVER

Markings:
On left side of barrel: ALLEN & WHEELOCK
WORCESTER, MASS. U.S.
Allen's Patents Sept. 7, Nov. 9, 1858
Deep cut cylinder engraving

Caliber: .22 rimfire
Barrel length: 3"
Number of shots: 7
Grips: Walnut
Serial number: 295
Finish: Blued

Fig. 4

RIMFIRE POCKET REVOLVER

Markings:
On left side of barrel: ALLEN & WHEELOCK
WORCESTER, MASS. U.S.
Allen's Patents Sept. 7, Nov. 9, 1858
Deep cut cylinder engraving

Caliber: .22 rimfire
Barrel length: 2½"
Number of shots: 7
Grips: Walnut
Serial number: 583
Finish: Blued

119

Fig. 5

SINGLESHOT RIMFIRE PISTOLS

Markings:
  On left side of barrel: ALLEN & WHEELOCK
    WORCESTER, MASS.
  Distinctive features: Frame does not extend over breech
    and no patent dates

Caliber: .30 rimfire
Barrel length: 3$\frac{15}{16}$"
Number of shots: 1
Grips: Walnut
Serial number: 993
Finish: Blued

Fig. 6

SIDEHAMMER RIMFIRE REVOLVER

Markings:
  Left side of barrel: ALLEN & WHEELOCK
    WORCESTER, MASS. U.S.
    Allen's Patents Sept. 7, Nov. 9, 1858
  Distinctive feature: Cased in gutta percha case
    Deep cut cylinder engraving

Caliber: .22 rimfire
Barrel length: 2½"
Number of shots: 7
Grips: Walnut
Serial number: 829
Finish: Blued

Fig. 7

SIDE HAMMER PERCUSSION REVOLVER

Markings:
  On left side of barrel: ALLEN & WHEELOCK
    WORCESTER, MASS. U.S.
    Allen's Patents Jan. 13, Dec. 15, 1857, Sept. 7, 1858
    Deep cut cylinder engraving

Caliber: .28 percussion
Barrel length: 2⅞"
Number of shots: 5
Grips: Walnut
Serial number: 908
Finish: Blued barrel, cylinder and frame, case-
    hardened hammer and loading lever

Fig. 8

SIDE HAMMER PERCUSSION REVOLVER

Markings:
  On left side of barrel: ALLEN & WHEELOCK
    WORCESTER, MASS. U.S.
    Allen's Patents Jan. 13, Dec. 15, 1857, Sept. 7, 1858
    Deep cut cylinder engraving

Caliber: .31 percussion
Barrel length: 3⅞"
Number of shots: 5
Grips: Walnut
Serial number: 724
Finish: Blued barrel, frame and cylinder,
    casehardened hammer

Fig. 9

DRAGOON SIZE PEPPERBOX

Markings:
On barrel flute: ALLEN & WHEELOCK
On left side of hammer: Patented April 16, 1845
Distinctive feature: Spur on trigger guard

Caliber: .36 percussion
Barrel length: 6″
Number of shots: 6
Grips: Walnut
Serial number: 29
Finish: Blued

Fig. 10

ALLEN & WHEELOCK PEPPERBOX

Markings:
On barrel flute: ALLEN & WHEELOCK
On left side of barrel: Patented April 16, 1845

Caliber: .31 percussion
Barrel length: 4″
Number of shots: 6
Grips: Walnut
Serial number: 220
Finish: Blued

Fig. 11

CENTER HAMMER SINGLE SHOT PERCUSSION PISTOL

Markings:
On top of barrel flat: ALLEN & WHEELOCK
Distinctive feature: No patent dates

Caliber: .31 percussion
Barrel length: 8″
Number of shots: 1
Serial number: 137
Finish: Blued

Fig. 12

DOUBLE BARREL, SINGLE TRIGGER, PERCUSSION PISTOL

Markings:
In flute on top of barrels: ALLEN & WHEELOCK
Distinctive feature: Two hammers and single trigger

Caliber: .34 percussion
Barrel length: 5⅞″
Number of shots: 2
Grips: Walnut
Serial number: 927
Finish: Blued

121

Fig. 13

BAR HAMMER PERCUSSION REVOLVER

Markings:
On left side of barrel: ALLEN & WHEELOCK
WORCESTER, MASS. U.S.
Allen's Patent April 16, 1845
Deep cut cylinder engraving

Fig. 14

BAR HAMMER PERCUSSION REVOLVER

Markings:
On top strap over cylinder: ALLEN & WHEELOCK
On left side of hammer: Patented April 16, 1845
Distinctive feature: Early variation with name on topstrap

Caliber: .28 percussion
Barrel length: 2⅜"
Number of shots: 5
Grips: Walnut
Serial number: 751
Finish: Blued

Caliber: .31 percussion
Barrel length: 3"
Number of shots: 5
Grips: Walnut
Serial number: 459
Finish: Blued

Guidance for the Collectors

"Caution" is the key word for gun collectors, whether they be amateur or professional. When any thing takes on enough importance to become a collector's item of any value, including anything from stamps to steam boats, the fakers and forgers are soon on the job. When you have paid your hard earned cash for a particular weapon to fit into your collection, only to find later that it is not the original piece that you were led to believe it was by the seller, or the seller was shrewd enough not to commit himself concerning the weapon's authenticity, you have that lonely, dejected feeling that this writer has experienced many times. The shrewd merchant of the "doctored" gun will assist you in your disregard for caution by telling you that if you are interested, you should go ahead and buy it since there are several others who are interested in the gun, and who may buy it at any minute. However, if for some reason you do choose to pass it up, you will, in all probability, have many more chances to buy it.

When buying antique guns, if, after careful examination, you think the piece looks good, take one further precaution and get the opinion of a reputable gun collector. There is usually one nearby since most antique gun dealing is done at the collectors meetings. If it is a mail order, there is an unwritten law among collectors and dealers allowing the purchaser a three day inspection privilege, and allowing the weapon to be returned if it is not satisfactory. The opinion of the experienced collector, in all probability, will be a very honest one, partly because he himself has been taken, and would spare anyone else the same fate.

After you have purchased something that is a fake, you

may as well bury it and charge it up to experience because it is doubtful, through honest dealings, that you will be able to move it. Also, it is damaging to your reputation for another collector to see that you have displayed it for sale.

The value of antique guns is affected by two factors: supply and demand. Although all antique guns are relatively scarce, some still go begging for a buyer and sell today for prices less than they sold for new. Others seem to command fantastic prices, but this is partly due to the fact that gun collecting in America is a rather new venture. It has come into its own just since the second world war. There is little to guide the collector on many items produced in America a hundred or more years ago. Research and publications are needed; the new collector can find a buying guide for most antique firearms in the *Gun Report*, (a monthly publication), under antique gun prices, and also by refering to the latest edition of *The Gun Collector's Handbook of Values* by Charles Edward Chappel. This book is very comprehensive due to the increasing interest in gun collecting. It is revised every few years to keep up with the climbing prices, and it is very profitable to subscribe to several dealer's catalogues for price comparisons, as well as to make an occasional purchase.

"Condition" This word does not mean as much in any usage as in description of antiques and the establishment of their values. An antique pistol in "mint unfired" condition will sell for as much as five times more than the same identical pistol in "fair" condition.

Many dealers will use the "mint unfired" condition to describe the best available specimen.

The next term would be "fine" condition. This means that the gun has approximately three fourths of the original finish, and is in perfect working order.

Then we have "very good" condition; a gun which retains some original finish and all its parts are original.

"Good" condition is a gun of good working order, but has no original finish and probably some roughness and pitting.

It is hoped that the preceeding will assist you in determining the condition of prospective purchases and sales.

The author would suggest that the beginner steer clear of re-finished guns. A "multitude of sins" can be covered up by a new bluing job or various types of plating processes. Once you have acquired a refinished gun, you will find it very difficult to dispose of it unless you are willing to sell it at considerable loss.